Emma—

BOUND

BOOK ONE IN THE FORBIDDEN SERIES

by Melody Anne

Dance like
nobody's watching!!

Melody Anne ♥

COPYRIGHT

© 2014 Melody Anne

Printed and published in the United States of America.

Published by Gossamer Publishing Company

Editing by Nicole and Alison

DEDICATION

THIS BOOK IS dedicated to my friend Mary, who is always eager and excited to be my first beta reader, and who has such a love of romance and knows my characters better than I do.

NOTE FROM THE AUTHOR

THIS SUMMER HAS been so wonderful. I've enjoyed my writing while out on the deck and in my motor home while on trips with family and friends. I love my job and love that you love my books, so I can continue doing it. I've engaged in many fun activities this summer and have been writing things down about everything. I always tell everyone nothing is safe with me. It WILL end up in a book.

Thanks, of course, to all of you who make it possible for me to do what I do! I love my fans, my friends, my family, and those who feel like family. Thank you to the members of my amazing team, who make it possible for me to write while they take care of business: Eddie, Adam and Jeff, and my cook, Sam, whom I can't live without! You all know how much I love my girls, who sit down with me for hours, helping me come up with scenes, the steamier the better, and who inspire me to write romance: my daughter, Phoenix, and Kathiey, Krisi, Nikki, Steph, Mary, and my sister Patsy. Thanks to Mike, who inspires me by how much he loves his family, and by what a loyal and honest friend he has become to me. Thanks to Dennis and Chris for help with matters of aviation, and to Chris for the scenes he doesn't know about — the scene in which we learn that Tyler once received an electric shock while messing with wires and the scene involving his broken finger are both based on things that happened to Chris. If it's any consolation to him, his pain has given me great writing material. Ah, nothing like tough guys! Thanks to my husband, who rarely sees me because I am working so much, and to my friends, who drag me from the house to make sure I have fun. Ah, and I am eternally grateful to country music, where there's a story in every song. I hope you all have a wonderful rest of the year.

Melody Anne

BOOKS BY MELODY ANNE

BILLIONAIRE BACHELORS
*The Billionaire Wins the Game
*The Billionaire's Dance
*The Billionaire Falls
*The Billionaire's Marriage Proposal
*Blackmailing the Billionaire
*Runaway Heiress
*The Billionaire's Final Stand
*Unexpected Treasure
*Hidden Treasure
*Holiday Treasure

BABY FOR THE BILLIONAIRE

+The Tycoon's Revenge

+The Tycoon's Vacation

+The Tycoon's Proposal

+The Tycoon's Secret

+The Lost Tycoon

RISE OF THE DARK ANGEL

-Midnight Fire – Rise of the Dark Angel – Book One

-Midnight Moon – Rise of the Dark Angel – Book Two

-Midnight Storm – Rise of the Dark Angel – Book Three

-Midnight Eclipse – Rise of the Dark Angel – Book Four – **Coming Soon**

SURRENDER

=Surrender – Book One

=Submit – Book Two

=Seduced – Book Three

=Scorched – Book Four

FORBIDDEN SERIES

+Bound – Book One

+Broken – Book Two

+Betrayed – Book Three

+Burned – Book Four – **March 2015**

HEROES SERIES

-Safe in his arms – Novella – *Baby it's Cold Outside* Anthology

-Her Unexpected Hero – Book One – Feb 24, 2015

-Who I am with you – Novella – **April 27, 2015**

-Her Hometown Hero – Book Two –**June 30, 2015**

-Following Her – Novella – **September 14th 2015**
-Her Forever Hero – Book Three – **March 2016**

PRELUDE

TAKE OFF YOUR clothes."

Jewell looked at Blake as if he'd lost his mind. "What?"

His eyes narrowed. "Take off your clothes. Do not make me repeat myself again." He stood back and looked at her through silver eyes that seemed to see right into her soul.

"I c…can't. We're in a parking garage," she stammered. She looked desperately around at the full lot.

Sure, this corner happened to be dark, but what if someone drove in? What if a police car cruised by again? There was no way she could do what he was ordering her to.

Blake just waited in silence, leaning against the front of his car and watching her pace nervously in front of him.

"Please?" Sheesh. She was reduced to begging now.

"I guess our agreement is finished, then." He shrugged as if he didn't care.

Was he bluffing? Could she take the chance? Her stomach knotted painfully as she weighed her options.

Wanting more than anything to walk away, she closed her eyes and saw her brother's sweet, impish face. What was she

willing to do for him?
    Anything.

CHAPTER ONE

I'M PLEASED WE'RE now business partners. I think this venture will be a success."

Blake Knight laughed as he shook hands with Rafe Palazzo, gratified that the man had finally come to visit from San Francisco. Though Blake had known Rafe for many years, this was the first project the two of them had paired up on. The contracts were signed, and the deal would put a few more hundreds of millions into both of their already fat wallets.

"I don't think there's a venture out there with your name on it that isn't a success, Rafe."

"Ah, my friend, the same can be said about what you and your brothers do," Rafe replied without missing a beat.

"We're just that damn good, I guess," Blake said.

Though at first glance the two of them might come off as smug and self-satisfied, and they might look at multimillion-dollar investments the same way an average person looked at depositing twenty dollars into their savings account, the men were shrewd and their self-assessments were based on solid fact, not ego. They knew how to make money, and they knew they'd always keep making more.

Only a select few ruled the world, and when Blake Knight was a young boy and his parents' lives ended right before his very eyes, he'd decided right then that he would never be vulnerable again. He would never be one of the weak, never be easy prey to a world packed with predators. No one would sneak up on him and catch him unaware.

"Let's have a drink, and you can fill me in on what you've been doing for the past year," Rafe told Blake. "Too much time has gone by since our last visit."

The two of them moved toward the conference room doors at Knight Construction.

"You're the one who sold your soul to a woman and disappeared," Blake reminded his friend.

"Don't knock it, Blake. Ari has changed my life and made me a better man."

"Oh, please, *please*, for the love of all that's holy, do not continue," Blake said, horrified to hear these words coming from a man who was once one of the most ruthless bachelors he'd ever met. "I remember the days when you thought no woman was true, no woman could ever be trusted. Marriage — your second marriage — has ruined you. There's a term for it, you know…"

"There was a time, Blake, when I would have thrown you up against a wall for just thinking me the slightest bit weak."

"Ha! You would have tried," Blake said.

Neither of them was remotely upset by the exchange, of course. It was all friendly banter.

Rafe smiled and spoke reflectively. "I came to realize that the anger I'd held onto for too long was pointless. I also realized that having one woman to love didn't end my life or my freedom. It made everything better. Ari is full of surprises and delights that I'll never get tired of exploring. I know you'll scoff at such talk, but what she does for me is indescribable."

"Yeah, whatever, Rafe — and thanks for not describing it. I happen to be a big fan of variety. After a few weeks, anything gets old, and women are no exception. I always grow bored with them — always! Besides, though I know it's not politically correct to say this, face it: women are weak, pathetic creatures, and they always have an agenda. Once I've broken their spirit, there's no more fun to be had with the relationship."

Rafe knew the horror that Blake and his brothers had suffered together when their mother's little game hadn't ended the way she'd wanted it to end. The woman had hardened his friend's heart, and though Blake was letting his resentment toward one woman carry over to all of them, it was somewhat understandable, if not right or rational. Hell, Rafe had done the same thing after his first wife's betrayal. So he knew there was hope. Time would eventually change Blake because he was fundamentally a good man.

"Not every woman is like your mother, Blake. You'll see that someday." Before Blake could say anything, Rafe went off on a slight tangent. "Who are you seeing now?"

The two men had made it to the lobby of the building and were stepping out onto a busy Seattle sidewalk. They were heading toward a favorite bar of Blake's.

"No one at the moment. I just haven't had time — all of these deals to be closed. You know the drill. I've had to do a lot of the work here on my own with my brother Byron being off in Greece for the past year, and my other brother, Tyler, gone two years. Now that they are home, I may take some vacation time."

"Now that's a joke. Men like us don't do vacations," Rafe said. "Why were both your brothers away?"

"Byron was working on his own project in Greece. He was

working with me on deals for the home front," Blake replied.

"It's good to branch out on your own sometimes, Blake. I would like to hear more about this from him. I personally love spending time in Greece. It's a beautiful country."

"Yeah, and Tyler was just gone for two years—we don't know where, and we didn't hear from him. I was about to send out the marines, but he finally came home."

"Now that sounds like a story," Rafe said.

Before Blake was able to give Rafe any details, the two men were interrupted.

"Rafe. Blake. How are you?"

Blake turned to look at Mathew Greenfield, a man who'd helped him through more than one bad time in his life. He was a business partner, but more than that, he'd been there when Blake had needed to choose which road he was going to take in life.

Luckily, Blake had taken a more positive path than the one he'd originally thought he would. Mathew had given him the support and praise he needed to change his life for the better — no easy feat, under the circumstances.

Mathew also knew all of Blake's dark secrets, and he was still someone Blake could not only count on, but trust fully, too.

"It's good to see you, my friend," Blake said.

"It's been a long time," Rafe told Mathew.

"Too long," Mathew replied.

"Join us for a drink," Blake said. "We're celebrating a new business venture." He knew Rafe wouldn't mind.

Mathew threw him a smile. "I have a few minutes. Why don't you tell me about it?"

The three men walked into the bar and proceeded to the back, where Blake had a table on standby at this same time every day in case he needed to conduct business away from the offices. A waitress quietly set down menus and disappeared.

Once the topic of business was out of the way, the conversation turned back to Blake's lack of a love life. That didn't make him a happy camper, especially since the last people on earth he'd want to discuss this with were teaming up on him.

"We all need to take time to have our itches scratched," Mathew said with a knowing look. "Have you heard of Relinquish Control?"

"What in the hell is that?" Blake asked with disdain.

"It's a place where you can get your needs met — discreetly," Mathew replied.

Rafe looked skeptical. "I haven't heard of it, and I'm not sure I want to."

"That's because you're a very happily married man who doesn't need a specialty escort service. It's only a couple of years old now, but there hasn't been a single complaint from any of the clients."

"I've never had trouble getting my needs met, and anyway…," Blake said just before the waitress dropped off their appetizers and new drinks.

"Yeah, but sometimes a man is just too damn busy. Relinquish might still be fairly new, but it's run by a very good friend of mine, and I promise you, you won't regret checking it out."

"Sorry, but there's no way in hell I'm going to a place like that."

"Well, here's their card in case you change your mind."

Mathew held out a nondescript white business card, and for some odd reason, Blake not only accepted it, but also found himself slipping it into his pocket. He told himself it was so he wouldn't offend a good friend and colleague. But as soon as he got home, he'd chuck the card into the trash. That was for damn sure.

"Why would you need to use an escort service, Mathew?" Blake asked.

"After my last divorce I decided I wouldn't marry again. And yes, Rafe, I understand that some people have great marriages, but I've been married four times now, and all I got out of each of those marriages was a lighter bank account and some gray hairs — hell, not even a T-shirt. A monumental waste in time and money. My great friend McKenzie Beaumont opened the place, and it's perfect for people who need 'companionship' but don't want anything to do with love."

"Blake, ignore this crap," Rafe said. "We've both been assholes for long enough."

"Believe me, I'm not interested." Blake picked up his drink and took a long swallow.

Mathew wasn't a bit annoyed at their reaction. "Fine. Fine. But I know you, Blake. You'll think about it."

The subject changed, and no further mention was made of needs being met. Still, though the night finished on a good note, Blake found himself feeling restless by the time he arrived home.

For some odd reason, he pulled the card out of his pocket and placed it on his desk rather than into the wastebasket. There was no chance in hell he'd call. No need. No interest, even. But out of respect for Mathew, he kept the card. It would soon get lost in the shuffle.

Two weeks later, Blake found himself staring at the simple black writing on the stark white card. He wanted to punch his respected friend in the face for even suggesting an *escort service*. It just wasn't his thing. And yet, somehow, some perverse impulse led him to pick up his phone and dial before he knew what he was doing.

It wasn't that he couldn't get a date. That was never the problem! This was about having his needs met, his need for control, his need — he had to admit it — for corruption. Relinquish Control's website promised through veiled hints that a man could get any kind of woman he needed.

And right now Blake needed a woman to dominate.

CHAPTER TWO

I'M SORRY, MS. Weston, but you haven't shown the courts anything we've asked for."

Jewell felt her legs wobble as she stood before the judge in her thrift-store suit, trying to tune out the sound of her little brother sobbing while his child advocate held him back.

"I understand that I don't have a full-time job yet," Jewel said, unable to keep from glancing nervously at little Justin, "but I was working part time until last week, and the temp agency promised more work, so within two months I'm certain I'll have enough saved to put down a deposit on an apartment. I already spoke to the manager of a complex over on West Street, and he guaranteed me a place."

"And where would you and your brother stay until then?" the judge asked in a level voice.

"I'm staying at a shelter." She knew she couldn't lie if she had any chance of getting her brother back. When Justin was little, their father had run off with another woman, and then, only four short months ago, he'd lost his mother. At the tender age of ten! In addition to all that, he'd been ripped from his childhood home right afterward and thrust into the unpredictable world of foster care..

"I am truly sorry, Ms. Weston. I want to reunite you with your brother. I even think the two of you need each other," Judge Malone said. "Which is why I won't close this case, and why I won't release him for adoption."

Jewell felt a spark of hope begin to well up inside.

But the judge spoke again, and his next words weren't quite as encouraging. "However, if your circumstances haven't changed by your next hearing, which comes in two months, I will be left with no other choice but to provide a more stable environment for your brother. He's been through enough, and the longer he's in the system, the less likely it is that he will return to you. He deserves to have a home, one where he can find comfort in routine, safety, and stability."

"I can take care of him. My mother wanted that for him — for us. She wanted us to stay together. The cancer was sudden, unexpected, and we lost everything, absolutely everything, but I can take care of my brother, I swear. Please, just let us be together while we work to put the pieces back together." Jewell hated that she had to beg.

The sad expression on the judge's face told her before his words did that she wouldn't be walking from the courtroom with Justin — not today, at least.

"This case will be adjourned for two months." With that, Judge Malone hit his gavel and rose before the bailiff could say a word. However the judge didn't leave the room immediately. He first turned toward Jewell with concern in his eyes. "I know you love Justin — I have no doubt of that," he said, and he sighed. "Sometimes, the best thing we can do for someone we love so much is to let them go so they can have a better life than one we might be able to give them."

He left Jewell shaking so badly that she was barely able to remain on her feet. But she looked resolutely into the sweet blue eyes of her brother and prayed she could keep her composure long enough to reassure him that they would indeed be together again. She went through agony each time she had to let him go.

"Jewell? Can we go back home now?"

Oh, how his innocent words ripped through her very soul.

"Ah, Bubby, soon. I have to do a few more things to prove to the judge that I can take care of you," she replied, disappointment thick in her voice as she walked right up to him and bent down to be at eye level. The advocate let him go and he fell into her arms.

"But why can't we go home? I miss you every day. Ms. Penny doesn't read to me like you do, and she makes me eat peas. I hate peas. You promised we'd be back together." His tears soaked through her thin suit jacket, and his small frame shook with each heartbroken sob.

"Oh, Justin, I promise that I *will* get you back. I'll do anything and everything for us to be together again. I love you more than the moon and the stars. I love you more than any other person on this planet."

"I love you too, Sissy. Please don't make me go back to that house."

"Ah, baby, it won't be much longer, and I'll come see you every single Saturday, okay? And then after eight Saturdays we won't have to be apart anymore."

"Eight Saturdays?" His eyes widened with hope.

Thank goodness he didn't understand that meant two months.

"Yes, only eight more Saturdays. And after that last Saturday, I will pick you up and you'll never have to go back to another strange house again." She would keep this promise no matter what it took.

"You swear?"

She was heartbroken at his question. How could any boy be so distrustful at such a young age? Her brother should be playing with action figures and Legos, not worrying about where he would sleep each night, or whether he would be with a mean foster parent or a nice one, or if his sister loved him.

"I swear." Or I'll die trying, she added silently.

"I love you, Sissy," he sobbed as the advocate shifted on her feet, letting them both know that their time was up.

"I love you, too, Justin."

His sobs grew into screams as the advocate removed him from Jewell's arms and pulled him from the courtroom. As soon as the doors shut, Jewell's mask of strength came crashing down and she collapsed into the closest chair.

When the court security officer told her she had to leave the room, Jewell stood and walked zombie-like into the cold white marble hallways of the courthouse. After making her way slowly to the restroom, she splashed her face with water and didn't even recognize the eyes of her reflection.

When her mother died, Jewell hadn't had time to grieve, because from the day of the funeral she'd been fighting to get her brother back from the state and the people who had taken him away. She and her little brother had lost everything in the last few months of their mother's life. But they couldn't lose each other.

Once she left the courthouse, Jewell wandered the streets of Seattle until it turned dark, and she slumped against a dirty brick wall, too tired to go on even a single step farther. So much anguish filled her every single day. Her mother had been her best friend, her rescuer, her only person to lean on and love in a world full of people who didn't care about her.

Closing her eyes, she thought of that phone call, her mother's strong voice, for once, sounding defeated.

"I need you to come home and take care of Justin. I have cancer, and I only have two months left."

The pain of those words still sat heavy in Jewell's chest. Of course, she'd come home immediately, and she would never regret her decision. The bills had piled up, the money had run out, and she and Justin had lost it all. Their home. Their security. Their mother. And now, each other. She wanted to give up, and if she were the only one she had to think about, she was afraid that she would.

She just didn't have the energy left inside her to go on. Wanting to stop feeling for at least a few hours, she waited and hoped for sleep to rescue her. For a few short hours she could dream, and with luck her dreams would be filled with images far more pleasant than the reality her life had now become.

How could dreams possibly be worse than what she was living through? They couldn't.

·

CHAPTER THREE

NO BIRDS WERE chirping when Jewell awoke. A light sprinkle of rain was drizzling down over her and washing some of the grime from her homeless body. She didn't know if she was capable of even standing at this point, but it didn't matter.

No. She was better than that. For one moment she'd given up; for only a second in time she'd decided it was all too much to endure. Now that moment was over. She had two months. As much as she wanted to break down and cry, as much as she wanted to curse the powers above for taking her mother, for interrupting her own life, and for ruining her, she knew she couldn't.

If she gave up, Justin would have no one fighting for him. And her mother's final words had been another plea for Jewell to take care of her little brother. Her mother had closed her eyes for the last time after Jewell had promised never to allow their family to break apart.

Her mother had found peace in a world that had turned against her, a world that seemed no longer to care about any of them. As much as Jewell wanted to take back the promise she'd given her mother, she knew she couldn't. Today would be the day she'd find a new job, save every single dime she made, and then get a place with furniture, in a neighborhood with a good school.

Today she would start the life she'd promised her mother she would live. True, it was all overwhelming — all the more so because everything had started out well for her. Although she was only twenty-four, had graduated from college only last year, she'd landed a wonderful job at an advertising firm where the execs had told her she was a rising star. She'd thought life would be easy from that point on. It wasn't turning out to be so easy after all.

After she'd chosen to walk away from her career to care for her sick mother and her little brother, her employers had quickly forgotten about her. When she came back begging for her job, they'd told her that she'd had her chance and she'd blown it. There were many like her out there, many who'd stood in line to take her place, and none of them would have let something as insignificant as family come between them and their careers.

That's where Jewell was different from the sharks in the world of advertising. Family would always come first for her, and right now the only family she had left was Justin. She wouldn't fail him.

When she saw a McDonald's, she slipped inside and headed immediately to the restroom. What she saw in the mirror horrified her. Her hair looked as if a crew of hyperactive mice had made a nest and settled in overnight, tangling it and leaving it filled with filth. Streaks of dirt ran down her sunken cheeks, and her clothes would surely have to be tossed.

Still, none of that was going to stand in her way — not today. After finger-brushing her hair as best she could, and rinsing out her mouth, she stepped back out into the lobby of the fast-food joint. Her stomach rumbled, reminding her she hadn't eaten in twenty-four hours, and then she'd had only a quick bit of bread from the shelter.

That didn't matter, either. She'd have plenty of food for both her and her brother when she found them a secure place. It wouldn't be fast food, though. Their mother had been an excellent cook, and Jewell had truly loved standing next to her in front of their gas stove, taking in all she was doing.

It didn't matter how good a cook she was, though, since she didn't have time or a stove, or even a place of her own to prepare a meal in. Even if she had to give up sleep, she'd soon have everything she and her brother needed to live a decent life. She would soldier on today without stopping until she had at least one job. She would work seven days a week, twenty hours a day if that's what it took.

Arriving back at the shelter she'd left the day before, Jewell walked through the doors and signed in on the visitors' sheet. It wasn't long before she'd had a hot shower, managed to find a small bite to eat, and then found a halfway decent outfit from the communal clothing closet to wear in her search for work.

The next thing she did was sit down and begin flipping through the classified section of the newspaper that the shelter provided to help people who were down on their luck. Sure, some of those living there planned on being in the shelter for only a day or two, but others were almost lifers. Jewell had been there too long already. She vowed to herself that she'd be out as soon as possible, and the way out was a good job.

But by the end of the week, she was once again broken. She'd trudged all around the city, job listings in her bag and hope in her heart, but door after door had been slammed in her face.

Overqualified.

Position already filled.

Come back once you have more experience.

Over and over, at each place she went, she was refused employment. What good was her degree? What was it doing for her now? She couldn't get a job as a secretary, because she was overqualified, couldn't get another job in an advertising agency, because she had left the one she'd had after only a few months and, anyway, she didn't have enough experience. No one cared that she'd left because her mother had been terminally ill.

They deemed that an unfortunate weakness on her part, a sad sign of unreliability. If she'd walked out on a job once, she could easily do it again. The truth was that she would if she had to. She didn't regret sitting with her mother, didn't regret those last precious moments they'd been able to share, and didn't regret that they'd been a family for just a little while longer.

But now she couldn't find a job to help save her little brother, and it felt like the weight of the world was resting on her shoulders. She'd promised Justin she would do whatever it took to get him back, to bring him home with her — wherever home was. She probably wouldn't be able to keep that promise.

She didn't want to give up, but it all seemed so hopeless. She just couldn't bear the idea of returning to the shelter, sitting through yet another sermon about hanging in there, about there being a better life out there for everyone. Instead, she found herself in an abandoned building she'd slept in before. There were other people around, all of them minding their own business, and Jewell curled up in a corner with a suit jacket the only thing keeping the chill from seeping into her bones.

Despite everything, despite her miserable week, she forced herself to be positive. Her last thought before falling asleep was that everything would improve in the morning. It had to. She would not leave the next place where she applied for employment until they gave her the forms to sign that would provide her with a paycheck.

Yeah, that worked really well for her. A week later, she still didn't have a job. She didn't have to give up on herself — the world seemed to have given up on her.

A shoe nudging her in the side woke Jewell up. She didn't want to speak to whoever was rude enough to interrupt the only time she was allowed a modicum of peace. She wasn't ready to face the cold, hard world quite yet. The birds hadn't even heralded the morning. But she slowly opened her eyes and squinted into the bright beam of light shining right on her.

"Are you alive?"

"Why should you even care?" Jewell snapped.

"Because I can see that beneath the grime on your face that you are a pretty girl. I think I can help you."

"What? What are you talking about," Jewell asked as she struggled to sit up. She couldn't see the woman who was staring down at her.

"I run a business, and I would like to have you come in for an interview."

It took several moments for Jewell's muddled brain to process the woman's words, and then she narrowed her eyes in suspicion. "Why in the world would you come to a place like this and offer me a job interview? Who are you?" Whatever it was the woman was offering, it couldn't be good.

"I find lots of women for my business in many different places, and I've heard good things about you from a contact of mine over at your former shelter. If you don't want work, fine. I won't waste my time. If you get tired of living on the streets, come see me."

The woman tossed a card at Jewell and then walked away, leaving only the sound of her heels clicking across the cement floor. It was too dark without the woman's flashlight to see the card, so Jewell just clutched it in her hand and waited for dawn's light to stream in through the broken windows of the old building.

When morning finally came around, she looked at the small piece of card stock and her brows furrowed. "What is Relinquish Control?" she said aloud.

Did it really matter? She'd promised Justin she'd do whatever it took to bring him home, and that was exactly what she was willing to do. *Whatever it took.*

CHAPTER FOUR

WHEN JEWELL STEPPED in front of the unremarkable building, she double-checked the address. It didn't have a business sign, didn't have *anything* indicating it *was* a business. Walking up to the front door, she wasn't sure whether she should ring the doorbell or go on in. Since there was no *Open* or *Closed* sign, she decided to go the doorbell route.

A year ago — heck, three months ago — the place would have seemed too sketchy for her and she would have turned around and walked away. But she no longer had the luxury of doing that. She needed another job and she needed to get money saved so she could ensure she would gain custody of her brother. Plus the woman had come to her, asked her to interview. So that was a very good start.

Jewell hit the buzzer next to the door and waited for what seemed like forever. A striking woman answered at last, but said not a single word. She just looked Jewell over with a swift sweep of her eyes before meeting her gaze.

Whatever this woman was looking for, Jewell had the feeling

that she'd come up short. Was this the same person who'd given her the business card? Jewell had no idea, because the woman hadn't spoken yet. She was wearing at least five-inch heels, doubtless an intimidation tactic. It was working to a degree, though nothing really mattered anymore except getting work. Still, Jewell wouldn't cower. She was going to paste a smile on her face and make these people want to hire her, no matter what the job entailed. There was no way she could suffer the disappointment of seeing another door close in her face.

"Hi. I'm Jewell Weston, and I'm here to apply for employment. I was handed a card and told to come by." Her voice came out strong, determined, positive. Amazing.

"I see you decided that you could do better than living on the streets — or in abandoned buildings." The woman's distinctive voice, with its low, sultry tone, was certainly the same one she'd heard a few hours earlier.

"Yes. I want the job." She didn't add that it didn't matter what the job was. That would sound too desperate.

"Come inside."

There was nothing in the woman's words or her voice to indicate whether she was interested or not. Maybe she was just bored with what she did for a living. She could at least introduce herself so Jewell didn't have to think of her as *the woman*. But, hell, she'd call the lady anything she wanted to be called as long as she provided a much-needed paycheck.

"What can you bring to us here, Jewell?"

They were now in a small room with a table and two chairs. The woman didn't gesture for Jewell to sit, so she stood there awkwardly.

"I went through four years of college and finished with honors," Jewell replied without hesitation. "I'm bright and always eager and willing to learn."

"That's a must," the woman said with a cryptic smile.

"Well, then, you have your employee," Jewell told her with a raised chin. "You may as well quit looking anywhere else."

"Hmm. We'll see."

The woman gathered papers from a file in the corner and then sat down at one end of the table, still without offering one of the chairs for Jewell to take. Should she sit? Was this some sort of test? The walls were bare, with nothing on them for Jewell to focus on to make her feel less uncomfortable, but she was determined not to look nervous.

"Where did you attend school?" The woman wasn't even looking up as she asked this question.

"I went to UC Berkeley on a full scholarship." Jewell was quite proud of that.

"Very impressive. So you are certainly smart." The frown between the woman's eyes suggested that she wasn't particularly pleased.

"I've always been at the top of my class, which is why I excel at any job I take on." Jewell had to close her lips to keep from saying more. Some potential employers wanted a lot of talking, and some didn't. She had the feeling that, in this case, the less she said, the better.

"Please have a seat, Jewell."

The tone of her voice indicated she *was* pleased Jewell hadn't sat down before she'd been asked. Good. Jewell was doing something right in this freaky interview. If only she knew what she was being interviewed for.

"Thank you," Jewell said. "Might I have your name?" She was through waiting for the woman to introduce herself.

"I apologize. I should have told you that already," she replied with a slight laugh that didn't reach her eyes. "McKenzie Beaumont."

"It's nice to meet you, Ms. Beaumont." No, it wasn't.

McKenzie's hands had long, slender fingers, and Jewell noticed she wasn't wearing a wedding ring.

For the next hour, Ms. Beaumont asked all sorts of questions that Jewell had never been asked before in a job interview, but the longer they sat in the small, stark room, the happier Jewell became. If she'd blown the interview completely, the woman wouldn't continue wasting her time, would she?

"Do you have family, Jewell?"

This question made Jewell pause. Should she lie? What if the woman thought her personal life was too much of a hindrance and then didn't give her the job? With a pang in her heart, she spoke. "My mother passed away a couple of months ago. I have no family left." It felt like acid traveling up her throat as she denied the existence of her brother to this woman, but she had no choice. There was no need for her potential employer to know about Justin.

"And friends? Do you have close friends?" What a strange question to be asked, Jewell thought, but she didn't care. On this subject she could easily speak the truth.

"No. I moved back home about six months ago to take care of my mother before she died. I had to leave everyone behind in California. I haven't had time yet to make new friends here. I'm not a really social person, anyway. I much prefer to do my job and then relax alone at home."

That was somewhat true. Sure, she'd enjoyed going to happy hour with her friends back in California, but her idea of a perfect weekend was sitting in front of a fireplace in the winter with a glass of inexpensive wine in one hand and a good book in the other. She didn't need an exciting social life. She'd been teased about that, though good-naturedly, of course. That *was* California, after all, where the game of life was all about being seen.

"Would you like to hear about the position, Jewell?"

The intensity in Ms. Beaumont's eyes made Jewell feel suddenly tempted to turn around and bolt from the room. She hadn't the foggiest idea what this woman would say next and she wasn't at all sure she wanted to know.

"Yes, of course. I'm willing to learn any job, and I guarantee I'll do it well." Those were the words that came out.

"Very good. We are an exclusive escort service. The clients we have like their escorts to be, let's say, *accommodating.*"

When she didn't elaborate, Jewell searched her mind to think of anything she knew about escort services. Weren't they places people could go to if they needed a date for the night who wouldn't humiliate them? Such as a cousin's wedding, when they didn't want to go alone, or a high school reunion, where they needed someone to be pawing all over them. That couldn't be so bad. They weren't prostitution places, right? She'd just have to go out on some dates. She could do that.

"I have to admit that I wasn't expecting that, but I think it would be fun to be a part of an escort service, to meet new people each week and to entertain clients." Jewell actually thought it would be far less than fun, but Ms. Beaumont didn't need to hear that.

"I am glad you feel that way, because we guarantee our clients one hundred percent satisfaction. Whatever they want, they get."

"*Whatever* they want?" *Whoa!* Jewell could have no doubt now what the woman was saying. This wasn't a typical escort service, at least as she understood them. Maybe other people associated escort services with sex and maybe she was naïve, but right now she was scared. This was a place that catered to the needs of men who would want things from Jewell she'd never before given *any* man.

Could she do that? Could she sell her body? She wanted to recoil in horror, to tell this…madam what she thought of her disgusting business, but the image of her brother's tear-soaked cheeks popped into her mind, the pain so vivid in his eyes. Was her "virtue" more important than his happiness?

"I need a job, Ms. Beaumont, a job that pays well. I think we would be a good fit for each other."

The gleam that popped into the woman's eyes told Jewell that she'd said the right thing. "Then you are at the right place, Jewell. Our escorts live here, and they go through a training period, paid of course, while they get ready to be the best they can at their job. Do you currently have anything you need to tie up before moving in?"

Wow! This was moving fast. Jewell wanted to run, wanted to hide, but it sounded as if she'd gotten the job, and she refused to run away from it.

"No. I can easily shift everything and move in," she said, happy to know she could escape from the shelter and from the abandoned building she went to when she needed a break.

"Perfect. Then you will start today."

With those curt words, Ms. Beaumont stood and walked from the room, leaving Jewell sitting alone, pondering what she should do. Was the interview over? Did she get up and walk out? She hadn't left a phone number with Ms. Beaumont — she didn't have a number to leave. So she waited right where she was.

After about ten minutes, when Jewell was wondering whether she could even get up and move around without endangering her new job, another woman entered the room. This one was older, with a kind smile on her face.

"Hello, Jewell; I'm Betty. Ms. Beaumont has informed me

that you are joining our team. Our bosses are wonderful to work for and I think you'll be happy with your decision. Please follow me."

Betty left the room immediately, and Jewell scrambled to catch up to her. When they entered what looked like a spa, Jewell's nerves had calmed somewhat. This really wouldn't be *so* bad. And maybe she could even work there for the six weeks until she got her brother, saving everything, and then slip away before she had to do anything that she felt would compromise her integrity. It really depended how long their training took.

"The showers are over there. Please take your time."

Betty handed her a thick, soft towel and then disappeared. Jewell stood there awkwardly for a moment, and then decided that a hot shower, one she didn't have to rush through, sounded like a perfect start to her new job. After scrubbing herself, she was then led to a tub, where attendants practically scratched her skin off.

She'd never been bathed by another person — okay, certainly not since her toddler years. Thoroughly humiliated, she had to fight back tears. *This is for Justin*, she kept reminding herself. Things got easier after that.

She was whisked into a room where what they called beauty treatments began. Some were painful, some pleasant, but all of them changed her in one way or another. By the time the various cosmetologists were finished, her hair was softer than it had ever been, at least on her head, because virtually all the other hair on her body had been painfully removed. Her skin was silky, her face glowing — and her stomach still empty.

The people who ran the agency apparently liked the women who worked for them to be nearly anorexic. That was fine, Jewell supposed — she was used to going without meals. Each time she thought she couldn't possibly endure another minute, she would just close her eyes and think of her brother. She could do anything for him, and if the brutal beauty routine was any indication of what she'd continue to go through, she probably *was* going to be doing *anything,* and *everything.*

CHAPTER FIVE

WELCOME, MR. KNIGHT. I hope you found us without too much trouble."

Blake looked at the tastefully decorated "showroom" and felt nothing but scorn. Why was he here?

The room was done up in varying shades of beige and red, and it sported expensive crystal chandeliers and lamps, though the lighting was low. Elegantly dressed women — no fishnet stockings and thongs were on display here! — sat and chatted with potential clients, their voices low, the conversations muted.

He recognized a congressman in the corner with a woman sitting on his lap and whispering in his ear, and the mayor in another corner, laughing as two women softly rubbed his inner thighs. Yes, the men wore shades and yes, they obviously thought the muted lighting would conceal their identity, but their arrogance wasn't lost on Blake. He certainly had nothing to lose if someone said he was there — the opinions of others mattered nothing to him. The place guaranteed discretion, and no one in the room seemed in the least worried that their secrets would be shouted to the world. After all, they were all there for the same reasons, weren't they? Curiosity — hunger.

"I thought the place was worth checking out," Blake said coolly. "I haven't decided if I will use your services." There was no use in leading this woman on, but if he couldn't even explain to himself why he was there, how would he explain it to her? Not that he owed anyone an explanation.

When he wanted a woman, he found one. It was that simple. His parents had died twenty-five years ago this month, and the anger that coursed through him on that account was stronger than any river he'd ever drifted down. That must be his reason for being here — an outlet for his inner rage.

"I think you will be quite satisfied with our selection," McKenzie Beaumont said with a smile that told Blake he could indeed have whatever he wanted.

He looked around the room, but none of the women captured his fancy. He'd clearly made a mistake. The women were all stunning, but none of them did a thing for him. And he didn't bed a woman without feeling a spark, without something about her making him want to take off his clothes — and hers.

"I agreed to come down here and look around. I'll let you know if we can do business."

He knew his money was wanted. Hell, it was wanted wherever he happened to go. He was one of the elite. That meant, of course, that his ass was kissed on a regular basis. He and his brothers were cynical, and that was okay, too. It was all just a part of the world they'd created for themselves.

The three siblings had learned from their mother at a young age to trust no one, not even those they should be able to trust above all others, and that depressing lesson had actually helped them. If they didn't wear their heart on their sleeves, didn't allow anyone even remotely close to the recesses of their hearts, they ran no risk of ever being traumatized again. That was the world they'd created. It was a good world.

Their greatest strength — their fraternal bond was paramount with them — was also a weakness. If an enemy wanted to get to one of them, he or she could do it through the other siblings. They would kill for each other, and they'd go to the ends of the earth, though they never spoke about that. They even tried not to think about it.

"Let me give you the tour of our facilities and tell you a little more about us, things that you won't find on the website," McKenzie said as she began leading him from the room. "We are particularly selective. Our women are, first and foremost, polished and elegant. No one will know you are with an escort. They are trained to be anything you need. We have a list of questions for you to answer, after which we will set you up with potential candidates, women who won't question what you want from them. Not only that," she said, pausing to look at him, "but they will also enjoy every minute of it."

"Then why the public display of your *ladies* sitting on clients' laps?" he asked with a mocking smile.

"Most of our clients are repeats. They like knowing they can come in here and be seduced. They like mocking society, flouting its rules — what others think of as wrong. We've never had any gossip or so-called scandal leaked from our premises and we never will, because no one comes through these doors who doesn't guarantee discretion. Furthermore, our women aren't for sale until they are ready."

"And how do you deem them ready?" he asked.

"Through a lot of training. Many of the women who start here don't last. They never see a client. They are put through many tests, and if they fail any of them, we fire them immediately."

"And where do you find these women?" he asked as a

woman made eye contact with him, and he turned away. Like the others, she did nothing for him.

"We donate a lot to the local shelters. Many women there have had hard times in their lives, and this is a great improvement for them. It gives them confidence and the ability to live a lifestyle they never before could have imagined. We don't advertise. I handpick all of our women. Not one of them passes without my approval."

"You call it *improvement*? They're selling themselves," Blake told her.

"We *all* fall on hard times, Mr. Knight. That doesn't define who we are. How we choose to pick up the pieces of our lives defines us. Remember that we all sell ourselves in one way or another."

Blake knew there was a story behind her words, and he found himself curious to discover what it was. But only for a moment. He shook his head, and the feeling passed. He wasn't remotely interested in McKenzie Beaumont. Yes, she was young, and yes, she was beautiful and composed, but nothing about her stirred his blood. Blake doubted anyone in this place would have that effect on him.

He was a hardened man. Or was he? He felt himself almost uncomfortable in this woman's presence. She had no qualms about her source of income — she seemed quite proud of it, in fact. Did she know what Blake had planned for one of her girls? Did she know it pleased him to make a woman weak, to break her very spirit?

Yes, he was sure that she did know, and that she even found some sort of sick pleasure in that knowledge. What should he think about that? He had reasons for doing what he did — reasons that he, at least, found valid. He knew it wasn't what the world deemed right, but he survived each new day by doing what he had to. His mother had done this to him, as had his pathetic excuse for a father.

The woman who'd given birth to him had been cheating on his father, her husband, and that's what had led to their death. Blake's father had been a weak man, and it was something that Blake was determined never to be. He wasn't the sort of man a woman brought home to her parents. And he felt no regret about that.

Blake was paying little attention to the tour of the agency's surprisingly extensive facilities. McKenzie had taken him to the spa room, where he could see a few women getting beauty treatments, their bare bodies laid out on tables, their eyes connecting with his as he walked past, no shame in their expressions.

He nearly greeted the looks they sent him with an open sneer. None of them offered him any challenge. He could walk from this place with any woman there, and she'd be more than happy to be on his arm, no matter what ensued. But would that be so bad? Maybe this was what he needed. He would suffer no feelings of guilt when he broke yet another woman, when he took his anger, frustration, and sadness out on her.

Not that he allowed himself to feel guilt — not ever. How he'd chosen to survive was no one's business.

When they stepped into a dim hallway and then out into a courtyard, Blake felt another flash of curiosity, but he kept it to himself. He was sure McKenzie was showing him so much because she was so eager to enroll him as her newest client.

Too bloody bad for her.

"Here are the sleeping quarters for our escorts. They do not leave these facilities without an approved client at their side. Once they sign on with us, we ensure that they stay 'pure,' in a manner of speaking, and protected from pregnancy, and that they have one priority in their lives — the men they are assigned to. They live only to serve our clients. I don't normally let clients into this room, but I am making an exception for you, Mr. Knight."

He wasn't surprised that he was being given the royal treatment. Anything less and he would have walked out by now. However, he was taken aback by the rules of this place, and that did surprise him. Not much caught him off guard these days, but this place was certainly beyond his imagination. Considering that he'd been to some pretty exclusive clubs, ones that catered to all sorts of men and their needs, he'd thought he'd seen it all.

They stepped through another doorway and he found there a room full of small alcoves, with only thin curtains hiding the entrances. Some of them were closed, some open, revealing women sleeping inside. He wondered whether the agency's escorts had different sleeping schedules, to keep an abundance of women ready for action both day and night — any time a man might wander inside in search of a companion.

In the large, dimly lit room, with shadows flickering on the walls, Blake's eyes were drawn to the different colors of bedding in the alcoves. Was that some sort of clue to who the women were? Red bedding for a seductress, blue for someone softer, more cerebral?

As he turned the corner, a woman sat up in her pastel-blue bedding, her hair mussed from its time on the pillow. She didn't see him as his gaze zeroed in on her, but Blake couldn't take his eyes from the dark tresses that traveled halfway down her back, or from the low-cut silk of her pajama tank top, which showed him just a hint of her tempting cleavage.

She threw off her cashmere blankets, and his next view was of her tanned thighs, toned and tantalizing, and just the right shape for his hands to wander over. She was the first woman in the building who'd inspired even the smallest trace of lust inside him. Hell. Small? What he was feeling as he looked at her was anything but small. He hoped no one noticed.

He tuned out McKenzie Beaumont as he waited for this new woman to look up, waited to see what would happen when their eyes met. If he felt nothing, he was finished with her and with this agency. But if he felt what he thought he'd feel, he wouldn't be leaving Relinquish Control alone.

Her eyes lifted and the room disappeared. Blake found himself taking an involuntary step backward at the power of the connection. Never in his life had he looked at a woman with such intensity. Never before had he been filled with such a flood of desire for any woman before she'd said even a single word. He would do just about anything, give anything, to possess this stranger. That thought should have stopped him cold, but he didn't hesitate to ask his next question.

"What's her name?"

McKenzie broke off in the middle of her sentence and looked in the direction his eyes had taken. He didn't notice the scowl on her face when she saw how smitten he was with this trainee.

"Her name is Jewell, but she's not ready yet. We've had her only a week, and we don't know if she'll make a good escort or not at this point. I told you that I guarantee discretion and satisfaction and I can't do that with her. She has some very good traits, but some things about her need to be investigated further." McKenzie turned on her heel and headed away, expecting Blake to follow.

"Jewell," he whispered, and the woman in question flinched, though there was no way she could have heard his voice from the distance separating them. He approached her and then knelt down so he could be face-to-face with her. "Good afternoon."

She said nothing, just gazed at him with widening eyes.

"Mr. Knight, this room isn't where we speak to our escorts." McKenzie had come back after him.

"Leave us." The tone of Blake's voice left no room for argument. He heard the sharp intake of McKenzie's breath and knew she must be seething. Though she was anything but a submissive woman, she had to follow her own agency's promise that its clients could have whatever they wanted, and so she did as he demanded and walked from the room.

"I said, 'Good afternoon,'" Blake told Jewell, this time cupping her face with his hand.

Her cheeks heated, and he was aware of sparks flying between them at his touch. Yes, the innocence shining from her blue depths had to be faked, but it didn't matter. He wanted her, and he'd made his decision. He let her go, stood up, and then he turned and walked from the room.

He'd seen all he needed to see.

Walking from the sleeping quarters, he moved down the quiet hallways, and when he entered the reception room, he found McKenzie speaking quietly to one of her employees at the bar. He had no problem with interrupting the two of them. When he approached, the conversation stopped and the women focused on him.

"Mr. Knight, this is Nikki. I think she would make an excellent fit for you," McKenzie said as Nikki looked up and met his eyes, her expression bold.

"No. I will take Jewell. Have her ready in one hour." Confident his wishes would be met, he turned to leave.

"But…but I told you she isn't ready. I can't promise that you'll be satisfied with her." McKenzie shifted uncomfortably, showing Blake her first sign of weakness.

"I don't care if she's ready or not. I have no doubt that I can train her myself — and I'll enjoy doing so."

"As long as you understand that I can't offer you any guarantees," McKenzie said, and then her eyes lit up. "And the cost for her is double, as she is new and you are her first client. I want the payment in full, up front."

"Yes, it's always about money," Blake said with a smile. "I will pay triple."

After writing out a check and slapping it down on the counter, he walked directly out of the building. He was done with negotiations. He had found what he didn't even know he was looking for, and for the first time in quite a while, he was more than ready to play. Training Jewell, pushing her, finding what her limits were — that was bringing him excitement unlike anything he'd ever experienced.

CHAPTER SIX

S HE WASN'T READY for this. There was no way she could pull it off. Ms. Beaumont had assured her that her training was nowhere near complete, that she wouldn't be asked to be an active escort for at least two months.

She had planned to collect her paycheck during the training period, and then sneak out before she ever had to go out with a client. Yes, she would sell her very soul for her brother, but if she could just jump through hoops and get out before she had to sell her body, that would be ideal. No such luck. The fates were against her, and it wasn't going to happen now.

Because one man happened to walk through the doors, one man who wasn't even supposed to have seen her yet, her boss tells her that she has one hour to get ready, and that if the client is in any way disappointed, it will be the last paycheck she'll collect. Yes, she'd get paid for this job, as he'd paid up front, but if he returned her early, she'd be tossed out on the street. It was a lot of money, but she knew how difficult it was to find work. She needed more to ensure custody.

The money was good — so good. One week with this man

— that's all the time he had requested — and she could pay the rent on a place for her and her brother for three months. She could do anything for one week, she thought in desperation. But if she kept at it longer, it would be even better. She did the math quickly in her head. If she went with this man for one week, and then another man for a week, and so on, by the time she went to court, she'd have the bills paid for a year. And she'd be free.

The best part was that the paycheck didn't show what she did. The judge couldn't use it against her. It just showed she had a well-paying job. She could do this. Of course the judge would ask how she'd earned the money, and that would be difficult to explain, but she had time to come up with something. The courts wouldn't find her a suitable guardian for her little brother if they knew she'd been working as an escort — an exclusive escort who wasn't allowed to use the word *no*.

Looking in the mirror at a woman her mother would no longer recognize, she had to fight the tears that wanted to break free. *Shape up, Jewell!* This was just another day in her life, a day she would soon forget.

"Your body is just a tool to use. It's not sacred. It's not important. All that's important is Justin," she whispered to her image.

"It's time, Jewell. Your ride is here."

Looking through the mirror, she made eye contact with Ms. Beaumont. If she showed fear, the woman would send her on her way, and she'd have nothing to show the judge. So, with great effort, she swallowed her doubts and masked her emotions.

"I'm ready." That was a lie — she would never be ready. She'd never be able to forget this day or what she had to do.

"Don't screw this up. I've taken a chance on you. I know

you aren't properly trained, but this is a good job and there's nothing to feel ashamed of. However we must survive, we do it. There's honor in that." For a brief moment pain flashed in Ms. Beaumont's eyes, but she quickly covered it and gave Jewell her usual stern look.

"I won't disappoint you," Jewell told her.

"I have my doubts. Just remember that if he is unsatisfied, this will be your last job with us, and I can be a cruel woman. I can make sure you don't find another job; after all, you will have to use me as a reference and I can ruin your chances." Ms. Beaumont ushered Jewell out of the room.

Jewell shivered in fear as they made their way to the back of the building, to the area where escorts were picked up discreetly. A man couldn't just walk out the front doors with a new girl on his arm every week. Someone might catch on to what this place was all about.

A large black SUV was parked behind the building. The driver's door opened and a man with an expressionless face stepped out, moved to the back, and opened the door for her without saying a word. With one final, confident glance at Ms. Beaumont, Jewell stepped up to the door and climbed inside onto the dark leather. When the door closed solidly, she felt as if it were sealing her into a plush coffin.

Surprised to find herself alone, she let out the breath she'd been unwittingly holding, and leaned back, tugging on the hem of her short skirt as the vehicle began on its journey. Never in her life had she worn such expensive clothing as now. It was all provided by Relinquish Control. The agency had an image of sophistication and class to maintain, and their escorts could go out only when looking their best.

Not that she'd be able to maintain the complete image when the next morning came around. Yes, they'd given her lessons in how to apply her makeup, but she'd always just thrown on a couple of layers of mascara and some lip gloss and called it good. The paint they'd applied to her face had been an ordeal, taking most of the time she'd been allotted to get ready. There was no way she could make herself up as beautifully as they had. She'd have needed the full two months of training and more to get up to speed.

It would be heaven to remove the pasty film of makeup, but then she'd have to apply the paint herself the next morning — or die trying. Ms. Beaumont had told her to not come from the bathroom until she was in full gear, makeup, sexy lingerie, jewelry. The props actually helped her. She looked at it like she was an actress and this was a role she was playing. So she would do her best to think herself into character and try to be the woman he wanted. It was all just so damn overwhelming.

At the end of the week, the director would yell cut, and then she'd be back to the escort agency, ready to audition for another script. Yes, she could do this, and she would give it her all. Making zero mistakes was the only way to survive until the custody hearing.

The SUV pulled away from Relinquish Control. As much as she loathed all this, she had to do what she was doing — this was no sign of weakness or moral frailty, no real reflection on her character, she told herself several times.

They hadn't driven far when the vehicle stopped. Jewell just sat there. Should she open the door or wait? As obedience had been drilled into her head for the past week, she chose to wait. If she was supposed to get out, the driver would come around and open the door.

When he did just that and held out his hand to her, she took it without hesitation and climbed from the SUV.

"Mr. Knight is waiting," he said, and pointed behind them.

The man who'd come into her alcove earlier was leaning against a small dark sports car. His sunglasses prevented her from seeing his eyes this time, and she was grateful for that. When he'd held her eyes captive less than two hours earlier, the sensations surging through her had left her stunned.

She recalled how he had caressed her face, and how she hadn't been able to breathe. It would be difficult to maintain composure around this man, but she'd do it. She had no other choice. It was either that or lose her brother to a system that far too often didn't treat children well.

Having mustered all the confidence she could, Jewell began to saunter toward Blake Knight. Her body language made it seem that she had homed in on him completely and that nothing else in the world mattered, though she was very aware of the door closing behind her, then the SUV driving off, and the noise of the engine gradually fading away. She was now all alone with the man who'd control her life for the next week.

Yes, fear lurked just underneath her skin, but she was surprised to feel some stirrings of excitement — something she wasn't at all willing to analyze. She didn't want to be with this man, didn't want his hands on her, didn't want to pretend they were a couple.

But she didn't find him repulsive.

That scared her more than anything else about this adventure. She'd been told over and over again not to grow attached to any of her clients. She was to treat them like royalty, give them absolutely everything, but she was never to even begin to fantasize in the smallest way that any one of them was anything more than client and master.

The men who engaged her services wanted a lot from her, but she wasn't expected to want or need a single thing in return — other than their money. That was the life she was choosing, and it was the life she'd accepted.

"Good afternoon, Jewell."

"Hello, Mr. Knight," she replied softly — this time she wouldn't have the excuse of shock for not answering him right away.

"Are you happy to be here?"

What a strange question, she thought. Of course she wasn't happy to be there.

"Yes. I find it quite a compliment that you chose me," she said instead.

His lips turned up in a sardonic smile as she did her best to look into his eyes, or really the lenses of his shades. It bothered her that he could see every little nuance of her expression, while he was able to keep himself hidden.

"No. You aren't thrilled to be here, but by the end of this week, you'll be begging me not to let you go. I assure you that our time will be well spent, though it *will* end."

She wanted to snap back, wanted to fire away and make a dent in his armor, but she wasn't allowed to do so. She was supposed to stroke his ego. That was her job.

"I assure you that there's nowhere else I'd rather be right now, and though I'm sure it will be a disappointment for me when our time ends, I will respect your wishes."

"Did you memorize that speech from a learners' manual?" He tilted his head as if trying to read her, trying to solve a puzzle and not quite sure how.

"Of course not, Mr. Knight. I find you very handsome."

"Then prove to me that you're happy I chose you," he ordered her, his voice suddenly severe.

She had no doubt that he was testing her, and if he didn't like what she did next, he might send her back. She almost wanted that to happen. Then, when she didn't manage to sell her body to save her brother, it wouldn't be because she hadn't tried; it would be because she'd been rejected.

As soon as she had that thought, she felt guilt eat away at her. Justin needed her, and she'd be there for him even if she hated herself. Her brother would never need to know what she'd had to do, and she'd have to learn to forgive herself for her sins.

"How would you like me to prove myself to you?" She hoped she was making her voice sufficiently sexy.

"Be creative," he said, still leaning against the sleek car.

Hesitating only another second, Jewell stepped forward and allowed her breasts to brush lightly against the smooth material of his jacket. That small contact made her nipples instantly hard, and her breath hitched. Maybe she wouldn't have to do much acting with this man, because he created sensations in her untouched body that were unlike anything she'd felt before.

When he didn't show the slightest sign that he approved of her attempt to be seductive, she leaned in even closer and ran her slender fingers up the sleeves of his jacket and then embraced his neck. She leaned forward and kissed his jaw, then trailed her lips across his firm chin and down the side of his neck.

Was she having any effect at all on this cold man? She touched the sides of his neck with her forefingers to test his pulse. It was beating rapidly. Yes, he wasn't as cool and collected as he was making himself appear.

That gave her strength to continue, though she was far from a seductress, and she had no clue what to do next. She'd just have to listen to what her body told her to do.

She never got that chance.

Blake's hands snaked around her and he pulled her tightly to him, then reached into her neatly coiffed hair, quickly loosening her locks so they fell over her shoulders. Grasping a handful of her hair, he forced her head back, leaving her far too exposed, and her neck a succulent dish for him to feast upon, as if he were a vampire.

This was too fast, too much, too soon. She wanted to pull away, but knew she couldn't. This was going to happen no matter what, so wasn't it better that he just take whatever it was that he wanted? They were in public, though. How far would he go with this? How far would she let him?

Without a word, he leaned forward and then his lips were crushing hers, punishing her for something she wasn't aware she'd done. He didn't ask for her permission to invade her mouth; he just thrust his tongue forward, diving between her gasping lips, while one hand moved down her back and then grabbed her derrière.

As quickly as he'd begun the kiss, he pulled back, and once her eyes fluttered open, she gazed at her own reflection in his sunglasses.

"You make me want to do things I shouldn't," he growled before turning her and leaning her backward over his expensive car.

He pushed his hand up her blouse and scorched her skin as he quickly moved over the mound of her breast and squeezed. The feel of his palm against her barely covered nipple had her coming undone.

"We're in public," she finally gasped, and he stopped, his lips turning down in a frown.

"Forget where we are," he said, and he leaned down and took her lips again.

She was tense for only a few seconds and then the sensations washing through her made her forget where they were. When he moved his hand down to the hem of her skirt and began raising it, Jewell found herself in the throes of a desperate internal struggle. Should she allow him to break every rule of proper behavior and public decency she'd ever been brought up with? Did she have any choice but to let him do just that? No. Not according to the agency.

"Excuse me, but the two of you are in a public place. You'll need to stop right away."

It took a few moments for the words to get past the fog in her brain, but when they did, Jewell was horrified to realize that someone — a stranger — was speaking to them.

Blake instantly stiffened and pulled away from her after quickly tugging her clothing back into place. She was afraid to open her eyes, but when she did, she felt the color wash from her face.

A police officer, who was looking anything but happy with them, was standing five feet away and pulling out his ticket book. If this incident went on record, she would forever lose her chances of getting her brother back. She was doing everything she could for Justin, and she might have blown it already.

"I'm going to have to cite you both for indecent behavior," the man said as he looked at Jewell with a trace of disgust.

"What indecent behavior?" she said before she was able to stop herself.

"The streets are not the place to have sex," he replied coldly.

"We weren't having sex," she argued before Blake sent her a searing look that told her to stop talking.

"Your clothing was out of place. I'm not arguing with you." The officer continued to write on the pad.

"I don't think so," Blake said, and that made the officer's eyes narrow.

"Excuse me?" the officer said, as if not sure how to react to having these two randy people challenging him. Blake then moved away from Jewell and the officer took a single step back, and his hand came up to rest on the butt of his holstered gun. Was the cop frightened, or did he just want to remind Blake that he had a weapon? Jewell didn't know.

"Get into the car."

It took a moment for Jewell to realize that Blake was speaking to her. She looked from him to the officer and decided she was more afraid of Blake at that moment than the law, and so, without another word, she moved to the passenger's side and climbed into the sports car.

She was surprised when she saw the officer's lips moving but heard no sound. Maybe the car was soundproof. If Blake riled up the officer too much, she certainly hoped it was also bulletproof. Too nervous to look away, she kept watching as the officer and Blake spoke. Then her jaw dropped. The officer put away his ticket book, turned around, and started walking to his police car.

Then the cop got in and drove off. She hadn't had to give her name, hadn't received a ticket. Who in the hell was Blake Knight? If he could get an outraged police officer to go away, what couldn't he do?

Blake entered his car a moment later, switched on the ignition, and the engine came to life. Without speaking, he pulled from the parking place, then jumped onto the freeway.

His masculine scent surrounded her, making her stomach clench as her desire immediately revved back up. When she noticed his fingers wrapping around the stick shift, she ground her thighs together and wondered what was wrong with her. This was a job, only a job, a job she despised. Being attracted to her client in any way made her pathetic.

"We'll finish this later," he said, making her jump in her seat.

"What did you say to him to make him leave?" She'd been dying to ask, but had waited until he spoke first.

"It doesn't matter; I know people" was his only answer.

Jewell decided not to say anything further. She had no idea what was coming next, but whatever it was, she was sure she would need her strength. Blake Knight frightened her — and, sadly enough, excited her as well.

It would be in her best interest to remember who he was, and also to remember herself. They weren't a couple; they weren't even friends. She was his toy to play with for a short time, and she was sure he'd make the most of it, take every advantage.

And then she'd be another man's toy. She needed to keep this sad fact constantly in the front of her mind.

CHAPTER SEVEN

"TAKE OFF YOUR clothes."

Jewell looked at Blake as if he'd lost his mind. "What?"

His eyes narrowed. "Take off your clothes. Do not make me repeat myself again." He stood back and looked at her through silver eyes that seemed to see right into her soul.

"I c...can't. We're in a parking garage," she stammered. She looked desperately around at the full lot.

Sure, this corner happened to be dark, but what if someone drove in? What if a police car cruised by again? There was no way she could do what he was ordering her to.

Blake just waited in silence, leaning against the front of his car and watching her pace nervously in front of him.

"Please?" Sheesh. She was reduced to begging now.

"I guess our agreement is finished, then." He shrugged as if he didn't care.

Was he bluffing? Could she take the chance? Her stomach knotted painfully as she weighed her options.

Wanting more than anything to walk away, she closed her eyes and saw her brother's sweet, impish face. What was she willing to do for him?

Anything.

If that meant she had to strip down in a public place and humiliate herself, that's exactly what she would do. But what if she was cited this time? Nausea churned in her stomach as she realized that Blake Knight wasn't going to make her time with him easy. She'd constantly be facing painful decisions about what to do, and about how far she could go without risking losing her brother.

Still, she had her pride. With a haunted look at Blake, she began undoing the buttons on the front of her blouse. The air was warm, almost too warm, at least to her, with only a slight breeze brushing against her skin. She'd soon be standing there in nothing but her panties and bra, the summer air dancing around her body, enticing her.

No. She refused to become turned on. He'd already proved he had the power to make her lose her thoughts, but she was just as determined to harden herself against this man, a man who was so remote, so cold.

She could be cold, too. She would defy him — if only in her mind, since she obviously couldn't defy him outright and still keep her job.

That was good enough for her, because she knew that she'd emerge the ultimate victor. She would get what she wanted, even if he was also getting what he wanted. But wasn't that what relationships were truly about? Both parties getting something from the other that made them happy, or made their lives a little bit better?

She did wonder what this man was doing hiring his dates. He was clearly wealthy, attractive and commanding. He seemed the type who could have any woman he wanted. Why in the world would he pay for one? Probably because the agency promised him whatever he wanted, and what he wanted was far out of the ordinary. That meant he was going to make her do things that would slowly kill her.

It was worth it, though. It would all be worth it in the end.

With trembling fingers, she undid the last button on her blouse, and she hesitated for just a fraction of a second before pushing the blouse off her shoulders and allowing it to fall to the concrete floor.

She waited briefly, hoping she'd shown enough willingness to obey him that he'd call a halt to this test, and she wouldn't actually have to strip completely naked. When he didn't move, but just stood there looking at her with those intense silver eyes, she knew her hopes were in vain. She'd have to complete her striptease.

Panic rose in her throat as she reached behind her and found the button on the waist of her skirt. Though her fingers were now shaking visibly, she somehow managed to free the button and pull the zipper down. She wanted to cry as the material slid down her body before she kicked it away, leaving her standing before him in nothing but her minuscule panties, lacy red bra, garter belt, stockings and five-inch heels.

"Everything but the garter belt, stockings and heels," he said, his voice deep — at least he seemed turned on by what he saw.

Oh, this was a nightmare. She was sure someone would walk out and find them. It was just a matter of time. She also knew that would please this sick, disturbed man. He hadn't spoken a word to her on the rest of the drive back to his place, but as soon as they'd left the car, he'd commanded that she strip for him. Was this punishment because they'd been interrupted earlier? It hadn't been her fault.

Reaching forward, she unclipped her bra and then pulled it away and let it float down onto the growing pile of clothes.

She couldn't hide her blush when the air touched her nipples and they hardened.

"Very nice," he said, and he shifted his stance.

She knew hesitating any further would only draw this out even more, so without any further prompting, she hooked her thumbs into the elastic of her panties and drew them down her legs, then kicked them over with the other clothes before she stood back up, now almost completely naked, an object for this man to examine with his damnably critical eyes.

"Turn slowly in a circle," he said huskily.

Jewell did as he said, wobbling only slightly in the unfamiliar shoes as she gave him a good look at her body. She knew it wasn't perfect.

"You're too skinny, but we can fix that," he said, and she wanted to slap him.

She was fully aware that she needed to put on weight. She'd love to be able to eat enough to do just that.

"Your breasts and ass are perfect, though," he said. "You will not change either."

She wanted to snarl at him, to demand that he give her the secret to keeping her body up to his particular standards and his alone. But she managed to keep her retort to herself. When she looked back into his eyes, she saw a hint of a smile in them, as if he knew what she was thinking and how difficult it was for her to keep her comments to herself.

That made her dislike him just a little bit more.

"Come here."

Her stomach shaking, Jewell walked away from her pile of clothes and moved toward this commanding man. Was she about to lose her virginity on the hood of his expensive car? She wouldn't put it past him. She only hoped that he wouldn't realize how inexperienced she was and take her back to the agency, demanding a refund for misrepresentation — heck, for a bad imitation of what a whore was supposed to be.

She had to pull this off somehow, no matter how much she hurt and no matter how much she felt like crying. She could cry later — when she had time alone in the shower, or when he wasn't there. There was no way he could be with her twenty-four hours a day.

Besides, she had to get away on Saturday, whether she lost her job or not. She almost had lost her job the last Saturday. She'd snuck out and Ms. Beaumont had been furious — and her fury intensified when Jewell refused to tell her where she'd gone. The woman had almost fired her right then and there, but Jewell had somehow managed to keep her job, barely.

This week it would be even more difficult. Blake Knight wouldn't give her a pass on this. He'd want to know where she'd gone, and when she wouldn't tell him, he'd end their time together. Saturday would be their last night together, though, so her week's duties to him would be fulfilled already. However she had other things to think about now; she'd have to worry about that when the time came.

After reaching Blake's side, she waited for his next order, feeling almost curious about what it would be. He reached out and touched her throat with one finger, and then moved it slowly downward, between her breasts, and to her stomach. Here he stopped and splayed all his fingers over her flat abs.

"Yes, you are beautiful," he said almost reverently, but the shutters went back over his eyes and she stood trembling before him. His touch alone left her barely able to stay upright, so violently were her knees shaking. The hitch to his breath as his skin connected with hers made her core pulse and grow slick in preparation for what she knew he planned to do.

His next command almost completely undid her, though she

hated herself just a little bit for it. "Spread your thighs."

She moved her feet apart as much as she comfortably could, opening herself up even further for this man and anyone else who happened to enter the garage.

"More." His tone was strained as she did what he wanted, spreading her legs as far apart as she could. "Now, bend your knees slowly, gripping my waist with your hands as you do," he said through gritted teeth.

What did he want? She was thoroughly confused.

Tentatively lifting her hands to his waist, she steadied herself and going lower and lower, leaving her core wide open, though he couldn't see it from where he stood.

"Perfect," he whispered, and she realized that her face was right in front of his zipper, and the fabric of his slacks was obviously stretched to the limit.

"Undo my pants. Hold me in your hands."

Her breath whooshed in. She was about to see this man, feel him. This was it. There was no turning back once she did this, not that she'd been able to turn back from the moment she'd set foot inside his car.

Without a word, she tugged his button free, and then slowly drew the zipper down. Excitement built inside her, higher and higher, in anticipation of seeing him. She should hate him, hate this moment, but she felt perversely intrigued.

Pulling his pants open, she freed him from the confines of his cotton briefs, and...*oh my*. Another, greater wave of panic seized her as she stared at the solid length now resting in her palm. She couldn't wrap her fingers completely around his arousal, and if he couldn't even fit in her fist, how in the world would he ever fit in her body? She unconsciously squeezed him, and was rewarded by a low groan rumbling from his throat.

"Make me come."

Despite his whispering, his words came through loud and clear, but she could also hear the tension in his voice. He wanted her to believe he was in total control, but this man, a man who liked so much to issue orders, was shaking beneath her touch.

That knowledge gave her more confidence than anything else could. Without waiting for his next command, she slid her palm over the slick tip of his shaft, and she used his own lubrication as her hand glided up and down its length. When his breathing quickened and she began moving faster, she knew it wouldn't take her long to learn what would make him explode.

Yes, she might not have done this before, but his sighs and his praise told her what he liked, told her to move faster, to brush her thumb over his sensitive tip, to hold him tightly in her palm.

"Your mouth. I want your mouth on me," he groaned, throwing back his head and breathing heavily. She leaned forward and took two inches of his arousal inside the warm recesses of her mouth.

As she sucked hard and continued to stroke him with one hand, while steadying herself on his body with the other, his pleasure resounded off the parking garage walls, and, even more encouraged, she took him deeper into her mouth. She felt him pulse, and her sighs mixed with his when his warm release coated her tongue and throat. His ecstatic groans sent euphoria through her entire body. She continued sucking him, intent on drawing out the last of his release, and then she slowly pulled back to look up at the man she'd pleasured — the first man. He leaned back farther against the car, and a sheen of sweat was visible on his forehead as he returned her look.

When several moments passed and her thighs began to wobble from the strain of her position, she wanted to get up but was afraid to do something wrong, something that would make him punish her by keeping her right there. As much as her body was screaming for something she didn't understand, she wanted out of this very public place. If she was going to lose her virginity to this man, she would much, much rather have it happen behind closed doors.

"Stand up."

Because her muscles were overworked, this command was more difficult to do, but she used his body as leverage and hoisted herself up, then took a second to stabilize herself before she retreated a step backward as he pulled his clothing back into place.

"You've done better than I expected," he told her before looking at her pile of clothes. "Get dressed. It's time to go inside and finish this."

With that, he turned away from her and began walking toward what seemed to be a private elevator in the corner. Terrified he would leave her there, she quickly threw on her outer clothes, clutching her underclothes tightly in her hands as she chased after him, adjusting her blouse while stepping behind him into the elevator.

Fear had become a constant inside her, but fear wasn't the only thing she was feeling right now — her body was burning with need, a need she'd never before experienced. Her thighs clenched together and she wondered what was wrong with her that she didn't feel any shame after what had just happened.

Maybe it was the circumstances of being where she was with a man such as him, or maybe she didn't think she should feel anything other than concern for her brother, but whatever it was, her heart pounded when the doors to the elevator opened and she stepped out along with Blake.

She feared that very soon she'd learn more about herself

than she wanted to. Would she ever be able to look into the mirror again?

CHAPTER EIGHT

THOUGH BLAKE HAD disguised his emotions like a professional poker player, he was shaken up. Yes, he was no newcomer to sexual pleasure — in fact, he'd thought he'd seen and felt it all. But when Jewell had performed her striptease for him, at his command, he'd had to force himself not to reach out for her.

He'd nearly lost control when she lowered herself to the ground and her sweet plump lips had closed around the head of his arousal. That just didn't happen to him — he was always in complete command of his emotions. He wouldn't allow himself to slip again.

He couldn't escape her tantalizing scent as she stood silently beside him and finished adjusting her clothes. Unable to help himself, he watched her out of the corner of his eye. Although she'd just given him a mind-blowing orgasm, he wanted more. He wanted to feel himself sinking deep within her heat, feel her body cradling him.

Yes, Blake loved sex. He loved all sorts of sex, loved how for ten seconds the only thing he felt was pleasure — no stress, no worries, no thoughts of yesterday or tomorrow. That was his haven in a world that had been less than good to him.

And yes, he enjoyed the buildup to sex. He loved the way it felt to caress a woman's body, to taste every inch of her skin, to hear her sounds as she was being pleasured. But something was different with the woman standing next to him. He wanted more, and that was unacceptable. She was basically a prostitute, a woman he'd paid for.

Most women were, though, weren't they? It didn't matter what their profession was. In the end they were all willing to use what turned men on to get an advantage, to get whatever they could.

He closed his eyes and was suddenly assailed by the sound of his mother screaming in pain. Snapping his eyes back open, he shook his head and forced out the eerie note of her dying voice.

It had been twenty-five years, and the anniversary of their death was approaching. He knew what that meant. He knew the next week was going to be hell. It didn't matter how much he hardened himself. Nothing helped. Therapists had told him that time healed all wounds — they'd lied.

Time did nothing but haunt him and he'd learned only to numb himself from the pain as a means of self-protection. Like the fight-or-flight response, probably. But you could run on adrenaline for only so long before instinct grew exhausted and couldn't be your savior anymore. What he felt, what he found to be the only answer to help ease the pain, was sex — lots and lots of sex with many women of all shapes, sizes, and colors. There were times he refused to have his needs met, just to prove to himself he could go without it. Only one thing was for sure — all women were like his mother. They all wanted to gain something, and in the end, they would all lose.

Blake was good at reading people. He knew who he should

go into business with and who he shouldn't. He also knew who he should sleep with and who he shouldn't. And he knew that he should send Jewell back to where she came from. Immediately.

He just wasn't ready to do that.

"Go and shower," he told her, needing a few minutes alone to regroup.

"Okay. Where?"

From her position in the entrance to his living room, she took it all in, her eyes wide. He tried to see the apartment from her point of view. Yes, it was large. Very large. Blake liked having a lot of space. Not much furniture cluttered it up, and he had absolutely no knickknacks.

The only semblance of an emotional connection in the entire room was a framed photo of him and his brothers that was hanging on one wall. Tyler had brought it over while Blake was away, and the pest had hung it up without permission. Blake had vowed to take it down, but it was in the exact same place five years later.

He was reminded of his unfulfilled vow when he saw Jewell gaze at the photograph. He didn't want her getting any ideas about him, thinking that he was anything other than a cold man with one thing on his mind. The picture showed him smiling, showed a softer side of him. That side wasn't real. It had just been a moment — a small moment in time. He rarely — very rarely, — allowed such things to happen.

"The shower you will use is up the stairs, third door on the right. That will be your bedroom."

Jewell jumped at the sound of his voice, and when she didn't move immediately, he swiftly loomed over her, making her flinch.

Good. He liked to keep her off kilter. He wanted to shake her from the innocence she pretended to have. Damn it for its deceptiveness. It made him want to protect her, and that was ridiculous. She didn't need protection; she knew all too well what she was doing. She could put on the innocent act all she wanted, but it wouldn't change where they would end up, and it wouldn't change the fact that he would cast her aside when she was no longer of any use to him.

"When I tell you to do something, I expect you to move immediately," he said, reaching behind her head, tugging her hair, forcing her head up so she had no choice but to look at him.

"I'm not arguing with you. I was just looking for the staircase," she said, a bit of fire in her tone.

Yes, he'd startled her, but she wasn't cowering in front of him. Interesting. He debated for a moment whether that pleased him or not, then finally spoke. "We could just head straight to the bedroom if you prefer."

Without giving her a chance to answer, he bent down and took her lips, then drove his tongue inside her mouth, desperate for another taste of her.

Completely shaken once again, now by the immediate current of electricity that shot straight to his groin, by the erratic beating of his heart, by the sudden blankness enveloping his mind, Blake pushed harder, trying to drive the feelings away. Lust he could handle, but he couldn't accept any sensations less easy for him to master.

Pulling her even more tightly against him, he plundered her mouth, greedily swallowing the groans she couldn't hold back and then raising her passion higher. Now desperately curious to feel his effect on her, he slid his hand inside her waistband and curved his fingers around her smooth behind before dipping them between the front of her legs and entering her wet heat.

He was indeed a predator, and it felt so good. Leaning back, he looked into her half-closed eyes. "You respond well," he said, mingling praise and a bit of mockery in his tone.

Her reaction was swift and fierce. She jerked back and — only because he allowed it — moved a step away from him.

"I'm just doing my job," she said before turning and leaving him behind, proceeding to the staircase in a measured walk, showing him that she wasn't running in fear, but going of her own free will, and paradoxically doing what he'd told her to do.

He took a step toward her, then stopped himself. He would let her have this one small victory. He didn't want to break her spirit too soon; if he did, he'd lose interest. He knew quite well that he could have her on her knees within seconds, begging him to enter her slick heat, but part of the reason he was so intrigued by this woman was that she didn't just roll over and let him have her.

Yes, she obeyed his orders, but he'd be a fool to miss the fierce pride in her expression, the self-loathing she felt for desiring him. He should be furious, should return her right away, but didn't he sleep with enough women who cowered and kowtowed, and with so little effort on his part? He was sure Jewell would succumb, too, but wouldn't the journey to her downfall be much more entertaining?

That thought didn't sit right with him, and Blake marched over to his liquor cabinet, poured himself a stiff drink, and swallowed it swiftly before refilling his glass. She had power, too much power, and he needed to take that from her, get it all for himself.

Yet he was enjoying her reactions to him. Damned if he knew why, but he was also enjoying the fire that seemed so easily to light up within her eyes.

Blake walked up the stairs, entered her bedroom, and looked over at the closed bathroom door. Hearing the shower running, he found himself wanting to join her, wanting to speak to her. What was her story? How had she ended up at Relinquish Control? And why in the hell did she fascinate him so much?

Leaving the room, he went into his own and shed his clothes. As he climbed into his shower, he decided against spending the night in the same bed with her. He wasn't in control enough to know how he would respond when he sank inside her, and he couldn't take the chance that he might be consumed by any emotion.

He really might have to send this woman back.

He almost panicked at the thought. "Not yet," he said aloud, shocked when the two words resounded off his shower walls. Now he was talking to himself. Maybe he should spend a day with his brothers. They could assure him he wasn't crazy or they could at least throw some light on what in the hell was going on with him.

As Blake got into bed, he wondered what Jewell was doing right then. Was she applying some of the expensive lotion sitting on her bathroom vanity? Was she slipping on the silk pajamas he'd had laid out for her? Was she thinking about him?

He shouldn't give a damn, but he wanted to know what was happening inside her head. He wanted to know desperately. He'd never before brought a woman to his apartment. It was his sanctuary. It was a place to which he certainly didn't invite strangers. That was thoroughly practical. If women didn't know where he lived, there was less chance they would hassle him when he was finished with them.

So why had he brought Jewell here? Damned if he knew.

His personal assistant had been shocked when he called her a few hours earlier and told her to find night wear and women's toiletries along with a collection of clothing that would be suited for any occasion. Of course Jewell came with her own clothing, but he didn't like the sort of outfits McKenzie chose for her escorts.

His assistant hadn't questioned him, and he was grateful that he had a semblance of respect for one woman in his life. More than a semblance, actually. He liked her as a person.

Now, if only he could find some solace in his own apartment. After fifteen minutes of lying on his bed wide awake, Blake knew the only thing that was going to help him was some intense sweating.

He threw on some workout clothes and went out into the hall. Walking past the room Jewell was in, he paused, his hand lifting toward her doorknob for only a millisecond. He turned away and went down the main stairs, then down another set of stairs to his home gym.

Turning the setting on his treadmill to a respectable speed, Blake ran until Jewell was flushed from his mind. Then, after climbing back up both sets of stairs, he rinsed off in the shower again and collapsed onto his bed. He was thankful when he finally felt sleep claiming him.

CHAPTER NINE

J EWELL FELT AS if she had sandpaper in her eyes. She didn't want to open them, didn't want to wake up. It had taken her hours to fall asleep the night before. When she was slipping on the pajamas she'd found laid out on her bed, she'd heard Blake's soft footsteps in the hall outside her room. He'd paused by her door, and she'd held her breath.

She wasn't sure whether it was from anticipation or fear. But when he continued walking, she'd let out her breath and slid onto the bed, her knees unable to hold her. She had listened for him to return, and a long time later, when she heard his footsteps again and he again paused by her door before continuing on, her body had tensed — just like before.

Only then had she finally been able to nod off and forget her troubles. Now, she was gripping the covers beneath her chin and forcing her eyelids together, afraid of what she might see if she opened them. He might be sitting there watching her. Though she knew he wasn't there — she couldn't explain why; she just knew. But still, she had a sick feeling in her stomach.

Finally, fully aware that she'd never get back to sleep, ever

so slowly she lifted her eyelids. She was on her side and facing
the empty expanse of the huge bed. It took a moment, but she
noticed a piece of blue paper on the pillow beside her.

She gazed at it as she worked on sitting up. Her name was
written neatly at the top. Did she want to read what it said?
There was also a small box sitting next to the note, and she was
certain she didn't want to know what it held.

But this is what she'd signed on for. She knew she couldn't get
out of it, so, ignoring the box for the moment, she reluctantly
lifted up the note and unfolded it. She read through it twice,
her cheeks flaming before she looked with disgust at the box.

What had she gotten herself into?

> *You did well last night, but you have a long way
> to go before I am pleased. I'll be at work, but I
> want you to be thinking of me while I'm away,
> so use the device in the box immediately after
> you wake up. Keep it inserted all day. Do not
> take it out! I will do so when I'm ready for you.
> You'll find a list of instructions on other matters
> sitting on the kitchen counter. I will be back at
> six this evening, and I expect you to be ready
> and waiting for me.*

Blake

Jewell picked up the box gingerly, with a *moue* of distaste,
and just stared at it. Did she really want to see what was inside?
Did he know she hadn't been with a man before? He had slipped
his finger inside her. Had he been able to tell they wouldn't fit
together? Was the device meant to help somehow?

That seemed the most logical explanation if he wanted her

to insert something *there.*

When she lifted the lid, she found a bullet-shaped device that had her blinking at it in question. It was really quite small, and that didn't make sense if he wanted to stretch her out to accommodate his impressive size. She twisted the thing in her fingers and wondered why in the world he had given it to her. And what would happen if she defied him?

If she did this, though, would it make sex with him less painful? How? She didn't seem to know anything anymore, and that was almost worse than anything else. She remembered a time when she'd been excited about the idea of having sex for the first time. Didn't everyone say how magical it was? Instead of finding magic, she was selling her virginity to someone she didn't even like — from what little she knew of him.

What did that make her? *Stupid question.*

Tears threatened, but she wouldn't let them fall. None of this was about her. She would do whatever it took to protect her brother, to keep her promise to her mother, who'd been a wonderful parent and her best friend. Jewell missed the woman so much that she still ached.

Yes, things could be a lot worse. Yes, Blake was cold, yes, he was demanding, and yes, she knew he wanted to take all he could from her. But at least she was attracted to him, even if it disgusted her to feel that way.

She picked up the "bullet" and the small tube of lubricant that accompanied it and moved to the bathroom, deciding she needed another shower before she did anything. Just looking at the device made her feel dirty.

When she climbed from the shower, the steam hanging in the air, she picked up the toy and applied the lubricant, following the directions that were included in the box. Then, standing before the mirror, she placed the tip of the device at her core and began applying pressure.

The pressure of it going inside made her stop. It wasn't pleasant, not pleasant at all — the metal was cold, too. She tried to pretend it was a tampon. She'd inserted one of those a million times, and this thing probably wasn't even as large. So it couldn't be any more uncomfortable, right?

It was just so demeaning, dammit. She grimaced as she started to push the foreign object all the way in. But she was so dry. "Come on....you can do this," she said to her reflection in a strained voice.

Gritting her teeth, she pushed harder and, with the help of the lubricant, the toy finally slipped into place, sending a strange sensation through her body. She shifted on her feet, closing her legs together, but with the toy there, it just felt awkward to stand that way.

After a few minutes, the foreign sensation subsided and she was left with just a slight discomfort, the sense of having something where it shouldn't be. Mission accomplished. She moved to the bedroom and searched her small suitcase for something to wear.

Once she was dressed, she began walking from her room and made her way down the stairs, the object shifting inside her with each step. Then, to her complete shock and horror, she began to feel an intense arousal as something bizarre happened. She stopped where she was and that's when she realized that the object was vibrating inside her.

When she reached the last step, her breathing grew slightly heavy, and her nipples were hard. If this was how she would feel all day long, maybe it wouldn't be such a bad thing when Blake took her — even if she did hate the guy.

She found another note in the kitchen; he was reminding her to keep the toy in, that he would know if she took it out for even a minute — and he told her she was to use the elliptical trainer, which she'd find in the workout room downstairs.

Why? She knew she was considered underweight, but she certainly wasn't out of shape. She'd been lifting her mother for almost two months, had been fighting for survival afterward for four more months. That last command irritated her, but there were worse things he could ask of her, so she decided not to fight it.

Just when she thought she couldn't take the toy any more, the vibrating stopped, and she slumped against the counter. Was it on a timer? What in the world was this thing and how would he know if she didn't wear it? She couldn't risk it.

Blowing out a breath of frustration, she took inventory of his fridge to see what he had to offer, then pulled open the freezer and found a carton of salty caramel ice cream. With a smile of defiance on her face, knowing he would despise her choice in breakfast food, she grabbed the carton and a large spoon, then took both to his living room and sat down on the black leather sofa.

Popping the top of the brand-new pint of ice cream, she dug the spoon in and took a large bite. She smiled in pure bliss. Heck, the creamy, delicious stuff contained milk and eggs. That, in her book, was a healthy breakfast. The idea of eating straight from the container made her smile as well. She was sure the uptight Blake would be horrified at her manners. But the "meal" and the way she was eating it gave her comfort. Her mother had always called ice cream food for the soul. It was a true cure-all, good for any and all woes, and it wasn't quite the same unless you ate it straight from the container.

As for the exercise, how in the world would he know whether she got on the stupid elliptical or not? After she polished off half of the ice cream and found herself more than full, she decided to put the rest away before it melted. Standing up shifted her toy and sent a current of electricity through her body that had her gasping. The vibrating had started up again.

"Oh my…"

After walking slowly toward the freezer — the toy was shaking her up enough — she put the ice cream back and thought about heading straight to her bathroom to remove the infernal object. But Blake would be furious if she did so. She would just have to deal with the extra stimulation for the rest of the day. Maybe moving as little as possible would help. Heck, maybe she'd even take a nap. It wasn't as if he'd know.

She somehow doubted her movement was what was causing the vibration. But she didn't know — she'd never even seen a sex toy, let alone played with one. Heck, she hadn't thought about playing with one, if this could be called playing.

When the phone rang a moment later, Jewell ignored it. The call wouldn't be for her, so why should she bother to answer? She was sure he had a messaging service, or he had his calls routed to his offices after a fixed number of rings.

The landline rang again in a couple of minutes, and she again ignored it. She returned to the living room couch to lay down. The sensations that rippled through her nearly made her tremble, and she'd been doing that way too much for the past day. *Whole lotta shakin' goin' on.*

Half an hour later the doorbell rang, and Jewell sat up. Didn't people who came up to his apartment need a special key or something to get into the elevator? Wasn't there security in the lobby? Who in the world would be at the door?

When the bell rang again less than a minute later, Jewell knew she couldn't ignore it. Still, what if she answered and it was someone whom he didn't want to know she was there? Would Blake become angry with her? So many hassles! She hoped she could get through this week without any more of them.

While she was hesitating, the doorbell and the phone rang again at the same time, and Jewell chose the lesser of the evils. She was sure she didn't want to speak to whoever was calling Blake, and at least his door had a peephole, so she could see who was out there.

When she got up and looked through the peephole, she saw a suited man standing there with a small envelope in his hand. Maybe Blake had forgotten he was having something delivered.

The telephone stopped ringing at exactly the same time as she opened the door. The man who stood there smiled down at her before holding out an electronic tablet for her to sign. "Jewell Weston?"

She was taken aback when he said her name. She blinked at him without answering for a minute, wondering whether she should admit who she was. That was ridiculous. Obviously Blake or Ms. Beaumont had sent something to her.

"Yes, that's me." She signed and then accepted the envelope. "Have a great day."

Once the man left and Jewell shut and locked the door, she went to the dining room and found a penknife. Cutting open the sealed envelope, she discovered a brief note.

Turn your phone on and answer my calls!

Blake

She'd completely forgotten about the cell phone the agency had sent with her. She was allowed to use it only when out with a man who had hired her, but as soon as she returned to the agency, she was to return the phone so he couldn't try to contact her without paying first. She was perfectly okay with that. But was he going to use her phone to try to harass her? Nah. No guy could be that much of a control freak.

When the phone powered up, she saw that six text messages were waiting for her. What in the world? Opening the message box, she found they were all from Blake. He'd programmed his number into the phone.

> You must stay in contact with me always.
>
> When I call you, answer the phone.
>
> Never turn this device off.
>
> Why aren't you answering me yet?
>
> Where in the hell are you?
>
> If I have to come back to the apartment, you will not like the results!

That last message had come in only two minutes ago. Knowing she would rather talk to him by text message than in person, Jewell quickly figured out how to type a response.

> *I didn't answer your phone because I don't live here and didn't think it would be from you. And I didn't answer the texts because I forgot all about the cell phone. I'm at the apartment. Haven't left.*

Within thirty seconds, he replied:

> Now you have the phone. Keep it on you at all times.

She smiled at the annoying message. She could almost hear the frustration in his voice, though she didn't understand it.

Man, was he bossy.

Yes, sir!

Adding the exclamation point was her salute. She wished she could give him another.

Ice cream is NOT a healthy breakfast.

Jewell's head snapped up and she looked around the room. How in the world had he known she'd eaten ice cream for breakfast?

Yes, I have cameras, and yes, I can see you right
now.

At that message, Jewell's eyes widened in shock. Of course he had cameras, and of course he was spying on her. Hmmmm. With a confident smile she looked around the room and then did something she hadn't done since she was a child. Lifting her hand into her hair so her intention wasn't quite so obvious, she stuck up her middle finger and smirked. *Take that!*

When two minutes went by and no further messages had arrived from Blake, she began to worry that maybe, just maybe she'd pushed this controlling man a little too far with her rude gesture. What if he was already in his car and driving immediately there to get his revenge? Should she apologize? Before she could make a decision either way, another message popped through.

You will be quite a pleasure to tame. Go do your
workout.

Ugh. Jewell wanted to scream. The last thing she wanted to

do right now was climb on exercise equipment. She had little other choice unless she wanted to get kicked out of this man's life and then lose her job, so she glared up at the walls of his apartment, hoping he was watching, and made her way down the stairs.

For just a few moments, she had forgotten about the toy still inside her. Walking down the stairs, even slowly, reminded her very quickly. It shifted against her sensitive inner walls and then immediately started vibrating again, and she found herself panting before she even stepped up onto the elliptical trainer.

When she'd programmed a workout and began running, the object continued to shift, continued to vibrate. Jewell felt pressure begin building within her body; her nipples felt like rocks, and the speed of her breathing had nothing to do with the exercise.

When she tried to push through it, the intensity of her sensations built up, and then suddenly, when she took a step, pleasure that felt like fire shot through her, leaving her nipples pulsing and a fine layer of sweat coating her body.

Her legs gave out and she barely made it off the machine before crumpling to the floor like a mass of jelly.

Her phone, which was sitting on the small table by the door, began dinging, indicating new messages, but she couldn't move. Lifting her hand in the air to assure Blake she wasn't dead, she then dropped her hand back down and tried to recover from her intense orgasm — her first orgasm ever. Man, had she been missing out! Why in the world hadn't she discovered this before now? The phone dinged again, and she just waved her hand again to the candid cameras and then flopped over on her back, a satisfied smile on her lips.

It took several moments for her to recover, and two or three more messages sounded off on her phone, but she didn't care. Let him come home and punish her, or do whatever he wanted with her, because right now, her body was on fire, and she was ready for whatever he could give her. Orgasms were weird things, like potato chips — you couldn't have just one, it seemed.

She decided she liked this new toy. She liked it a lot. She also decided she didn't mind exercise one little bit.

CHAPTER TEN

"HOW WAS YOUR day?"

Jewell looked up from the couch as Blake approached her. Exhausting! That's how her day had been. Thanks to his contraption, which she still held obediently inside her very tender core, she'd been pleasured more than she thought possible.

She wouldn't tell him that she'd also searched the apartment for any clues at all of who he was. Sure, he'd know that she'd been wandering around, at least if he'd bothered to watch all day, and that seemed unlikely. He hadn't gotten so freaking rich by being a voyeur 24/7. In any case, she'd come up empty. There was nothing personal anywhere. No photos except for the one of him and his brothers that he seemed to resent hanging on his wall. Nothing.

She'd even looked in drawers, in cupboards. Yes, it was a violation of his privacy, but he'd brought her to his place and then left her there to fend for herself. If she was going to be with this man for a week, she wanted to know something about him. She was truly out of luck.

Too bad his office was so tightly locked. Curiosity about what was hidden inside was still eating at her. That was where men hid their deep dark secrets, wasn't it? She would love to get in there. She'd bet all the money she had, which admittedly wasn't much, that there was something telling about the man behind that sealed door.

When she realized she was taking too long to answer him, she tried to remember what he'd asked. Oh, yes, he wanted to know about her day. Well, she wouldn't admit to him how much of an impact his little toy had had on her. Not even if he threatened to pour fire ants on her if she didn't confess. Still, to judge by the smug look on his face, he already knew. So maybe he had been glued to his computer screen, watching while she'd nearly collapsed almost everywhere in his apartment as each new orgasm had overpowered her body, sucking up any and all energy.

"It was fine," she replied, hoping she was as expert at keeping a mask in place as he was.

He gazed at her for several moments with those penetrating eyes, making her break out in yet another sweat. She wanted him, and again she hated herself for it. It seriously undercut her inner claims about worthy self-sacrifice, and made her actually feel even dirtier than she had right after she'd accepted the job from Relinquish Control. A hooker with a heart of gold? Hah! Try *with a heart full of lust*.

"I'll let you lie to me for now," he said with a knowing smile. "But I watched you all day, and I know that your body has been in a constant state of arousal from the moment you inserted that toy. I know that you are dripping wet and ready for me to plunge deep inside your heat." He put his hands on the back of the couch and leaned in, letting his warm, sweet breath wash over her face. "And, Jewell," he added, making her barely able to hold the gasp back, "I'm going to fuck you hard tonight."

He moved away and, removing his hand-tailored jacket, dropped it carelessly on the arm. His white fitted shirt showcased every muscle in his back as he unconsciously flexed his arms. Next, he removed his cuff links and was rolling up his sleeves when he turned back around to find her staring at him, stunned.

She felt as if she couldn't move, couldn't breathe. This man had nearly made her reach orgasm again with just his words and the caress of his breath on her mouth. She only hoped she'd be able to survive her week with him, because right now she didn't know how that was possible.

"Go upstairs and put this on." He sauntered toward her, a bag in his hand that he'd previously deposited, along with his briefcase, right inside the living room.

Jewell took the bag without question, though she was hardly eager to learn what he was going to inflict upon her next. She rose and ascended the stairs with as much grace as she could muster, cursing her body when she felt new moisture flood her lower regions, and her nipples jut straight out in the telltale sign of arousal. They'd been hard most of the day, but they'd somehow become even harder.

When she reached her room and emptied the bag's contents on her bed, she groaned. There would be nothing she could hide from him in this getup. He knew that, and he'd doubtless enjoy every second of her torment.

Discarding the clothes she had on, she slipped on the itsy-bitsy skirt — it barely covered her behind! Of course there were no panties to go with it. Was this another way for him to keep control? To keep her uncomfortable? To keep her vulnerable?

Next she fastened the bustier, shoving her breasts up high, her nipples on full display from the garment's daringly low-cut front. After slipping on the five-inch red heels, she turned and gazed at her reflection in the mirror.

Her skin was already flushed, her eyes bright with the pleasure she'd been receiving all day, and her body trembling just slightly. The outfit did nothing to hide any of this. He would know that each step she took sent shudders through her, know that when his breath brushed her skin, she grew more aroused. He would know that she didn't need to fake anything with him.

Should she even try? What point would there be to try to hide her reactions? Maybe it would be better if she just walked up to him, told him she was ready, and got the sex over with. Maybe after she was free of the stupid device, she would go back to normal. And maybe his game would be over once he possessed her.

Maybe she would be the next Olympic gold medalist in the category Lying to Oneself.

Carefully descending the stairs — she didn't want to put her insides into any more turmoil than she had to — she paused halfway down when she heard the doorbell ring. She felt trapped, not sure which way to go. Blake doubtless hadn't heard her yet, and she didn't want to be anywhere near the living room or kitchen if someone entered the apartment. As quietly as she could, she retreated up the stairs, and just as she reached the top, another orgasm pulsed through her core, causing her breath to rush out in awed celebration. She couldn't hold back the whimper of pleasure, but she bit her lip to prevent any further sound from giving her away.

Collapsing onto the upstairs landing, she waited for the shudders to subside and prayed no one had heard her. When Blake appeared below, his eyes dancing with desire, she knew the cat was out of the bag.

"Come down," he ordered, and began unbuttoning his shirt.

Holy hell! That chest of his was something dreams were made of. He was far too perfect looking to be the emotional mess that he obviously was. No mere mortal should possess such looks, such poise, such money. He had it all, and it wasn't fair to the people he trampled under his feet.

"Give me a moment," she said. She was afraid she might not be able to walk yet.

"Now!" His tone was firm as he made a show of letting his shirt land at the foot of the staircase.

With a defiant pursing of her lips, she gripped the banister and pulled herself to her feet, though her legs were still weak. She knew it was going to send sharp pains through her body to move this soon after another orgasm, knew that each step would be torture, but she didn't want him to come up and get her. She had no idea what would happen then. Of course, she also had no idea what would happen if she met him down there at the bottom of the stairs.

Taking the steps slowly, she tried to blunt the impact of the toy rubbing her swollen walls. She forced herself to focus on anything else than that. This was going to be a long evening if he made her keep the damned thing in the whole time.

"Sit."

"What?" She was confused. She had four stairs to go.

"I said *sit*."

Gladly, she thought as she sat with her knees together, squeezing her thighs tight, trying to give her body some needed relief. "Is someone here?"

"No. Our dinner was delivered. The woman who brought it is gone."

That's a relief, Jewell thought.

"Open your legs."

Her eyes almost bugged out. She wasn't wearing panties, and

he couldn't help but see the moisture coating her womanhood. She also knew that to argue would be pointless.

Leaning her head back, unwilling to make eye contact when she was in such a vulnerable position, she spread her legs, then braced her heeled feet on the stairs and moved her thighs even farther apart.

A gasp of honest appreciation from him brought on an extra surge of moisture, and she hoped like hell she wasn't dripping onto his polished wooden staircase. *So mortifying.* But constant humiliation seemed to be the name of his game.

"Damn, you are glorious," he whispered reverently.

Okay, so *that* wasn't exactly humiliating. With her eyes closed, and trying her best to do her *job*, she didn't hear him move, but suddenly she felt his finger rubbing from the top of her core, along her swollen clit, down her slick folds and then back up again.

"Push your hips forward, and grab the railing," he whispered huskily, and Jewell couldn't do anything other than comply.

When she felt the heat of his breath brush against her swollen nub, her body clenched with need. At the first swipe of his tongue against the bit of pulsing flesh, she jumped.

"Stay still," he said, pulling his mouth away.

That made her want to scream. A low rumble sounded from deep in her throat, and for the next few seconds all she felt was his warm breath again, teasing her sensitive pleasure point almost intolerably.

She wanted to beg him to go back to what he'd done with his tongue, but she couldn't do that. This wasn't about her needs. He needed to be in control. He needed to have her do his bidding. If he knew how tortured she felt, he would only torture her more.

So with all the willpower she possessed, she waited in silence for what he would do next. When his lips circled her clitoris again, she didn't even try to contain the moan. While sucking the little mound into his mouth, he simultaneously pushed a finger inside her, moving it around the toy still resting there, and a cry of pleasure escaped from her lungs as she convulsed against the hard stairs.

When she finally came down from the high, she raised her head slowly, and found his silver gaze burning into her.

"You are so responsive," he said with a shudder as he got up and then sat next to her, putting his face only inches from hers. She wanted those lips, wanted to feel him pressed against her. How could she possibly want or need anything more after all he'd put her through this whole day? She didn't know, but suspected that the games were just beginning.

He leaned forward and gently clamped his teeth down on her bottom lip and sucked, sending a whole new level of desire throughout her small frame. Just as confusingly as this sexual play date had begun, he ended it by casually leaning back and then standing up.

What was next? Should she get up, hold out her hands to him, beg him to take her to bed? No. None of that would make him happy. So, once again, she just waited. This was getting a little old.

"Time for dinner."

With those words, he left her panting on the stairs. She wanted to yank out the device he'd made her insert, and wanted to demand he stop toying with her this way. She did none of that, of course. Instead, she struggled up on unsteady legs and followed him into the dining room.

A table was set with candles already lit and soft music playing in the background. Why the seduction scene? She was already paid for, a guaranteed lay. And yet he held out a chair for her.

But when she sat down, he leaned over her and asked, "Ready for round two?"

Hot damn!

She was more than ready.

CHAPTER ELEVEN

WHILE PUSHING JEWELL'S chair in, Blake brushed her shoulder with his hand, and desire shot through him. He moved his seat closer to hers. None of that across-the-table nonsense of civilized dining for two. He needed her to be next to him, needed to feel the softness of her skin against his fingers.

The buildup, the anticipation, the hunger of playing these games with her — this was the greatest he'd felt in a long time. He needed to see how far he could push her, how far he could push himself. He'd never before had so much enjoyment with the preliminaries and actualities of sex. He would never have waited so long to possess any woman other than this one. Sure, the buildup always had its charms, but if Jewell were someone else, he would have bedded her the night before, and several times today as well, and he'd already be tiring of her.

This woman had him thinking twice, though. The way she held herself, the burning in her eyes, the confusion. She was a mystery and he swore he couldn't stand any mysteries involving women — why waste the time solving them? — but he wanted to know her, wanted to learn her story. He also wanted to get as far away as possible from her, but he couldn't make himself do that.

Jewell responded so well to him. And though he could see she wanted to hate him — if she were smart, she would — whenever he touched her, she went up in flames. Her body was a canvas for him to paint, and paint it he would. She intrigued him, made him think that a week wouldn't be nearly enough with her, but that's all he could allow himself to have. He had a feeling that if he tried to extend his time with her, it would be too hard to ever let her go.

When Sunday morning came around, he'd have her delivered back to her brothel, and he'd never think of her again. He knew he could do this — he was strong. She was just one more woman in a long line of women. It didn't matter to him that another man would touch her, do the sorts of things he was doing with her and more.

Then why did you bring her home?

Dammit! He didn't want his own brain arguing with him. He didn't know why he'd brought her to his place instead of a hotel room, didn't know why he liked the idea of her staying here among his possessions while he worked.

He'd never had the desire to bring another woman through his front door, and he strongly suspected that he'd never feel that way again. He refused to analyze the thought, however. Tonight was about sex, it was about pleasure, it was about taking from Jewell what he wanted, and giving her only what he felt like giving.

What made it so frustrating, though, was that he wanted to give her so much. Yes, he'd pleasured her because he'd wanted to, but he knew he'd gotten even more joy from her orgasm than she'd received. That's what this woman, this stranger, did to him.

She made him feel alive and excited. She made him forget about his past, made him forget why he'd gone in search of her. She made him think only of her. He would have to do better at keeping the walls he'd built up around him intact, because if he wasn't careful, she would have a hold on him, and that just wasn't acceptable.

"You'll have to do better at obeying me tomorrow," he said as he served up her dinner, making sure that he brushed against her again in the process.

"I did everything you asked today." Her voice was quiet, subdued, and he noticed how she shifted position on her chair. Ah, the toy had been getting to her the entire day, and he planned to use it while they were at the table. He loved the control he had over her body...and it wasn't just from those good vibrations.

"I saw your defiance, and I will force that attitude from you. Go get that bag there in the corner and bring it me."

She looked in the direction he indicated with his eyes, and then stood up obediently. He saw the tension in her shoulders, and he could tell she hated his commands, knew that it irked her to follow his orders like a well-trained puppy. She also knew that if she didn't do it, he would remove her instantly from his life.

He pushed that uncomfortable thought aside. So what if he had to fire her? He had no use for a willful woman. He'd chosen Jewell so he could be the one to train her, break her. He liked that he got to be the first man to take her from the escort agency.

As she picked up the bag, a shudder passed through her, making him smile. Every time she shifted, the toy moved, sending shock waves through her. He also controlled the remote that set it to vibration any time he was in the mood to give her a good jolt.

Wriggling in his seat, he welcomed the pulsing of his arousal, the hard state he'd been in all day. Because when he finally sheathed himself inside her, it would be like coming home.

She brought the bag over and stood next to him, waiting to see what he wanted her to do with it. When he did nothing but look at her, she shifted on her feet and then winced.

"Place the bag on the floor and then straddle my lap, but don't sit down entirely," he said, then cleared his throat. Desire was heavy in his voice.

"Like this?"

"Oh yes," he said as she stretched her legs wide, her breasts now perfectly level with his face, her nipples peeking out at him — and peaking, too! — above the corset.

He trailed his hands up the outside of her thighs, over her hips, and along the alluring indent of her waist, then ran them over the fullness of her beautiful breasts. The passion shining in her eyes was more than enough thanks for his attentions.

"Dance for me, Jewell."

She froze as she looked down at him. "I…I don't know how."

"Yes, you do. Move your body against mine. Make me want no woman but you." He gripped her hips and guided her.

She started slowly, her hips swaying as her feet stayed firmly planted. Then, after a moment, her eyes closed and she lifted her hands above her head, her upper body swaying as her knees dipped and she lowered herself, resting her backside on his thighs for only an instant, an instant that had him going from hard to complete steel.

When she stepped back from him, pressing her hand briefly against his chest for balance and then letting go, he nearly protested until she turned around, showing him her delicious derrière as she undulated before him, her sweet curves screaming at him, almost ordering him to take her.

When she bent forward, sticking her ass high in the air while spreading her legs and swinging her hips again, he felt himself begin to rise involuntarily from his seat. He needed to take her right this very minute. He somehow forced himself to sit back down, but he had to grip the bottom of his chair just to hold himself in place. He did have a motive for waiting — he needed to see how far she would take this dance.

Standing back up, she turned her head and looked back at him, desire a blinding light in her eyes, her expression one of both arousal and innocence. Yeah, right. He shook that off. It was an act, and she was very good at it. Still, by going along with her pretense of being untouched, he found himself wanting her even more. But before he could say a word, she turned her head away.

Don't be a fool, he said to himself. He'd discovered her at what was basically a brothel, and he'd bought her services. She was far from innocent — no woman was, when it came down to it. And he really wanted to come down to it.

"Strip for me," he commanded, hating the slight edge of weakness she was causing him to feel.

She ceased her dance for a second, and a shudder passed down her spine. Good. This was better. He needed to keep her guessing what he would ask her to do next. With her back still toward him, she lifted her hands. And he watched her loosen her bustier and let it fall to the floor.

His arousal throbbed painfully.

"Turn around."

She did as he asked, her hands up, covering her beautiful breasts as she swung her hips, continuing the dance that was just for him.

"Come here."

She stepped forward, standing in front of his opened thighs, her minuscule skirt hiding nothing from him.

"Closer."

She was shaking as she stepped up flush against his body, her breasts right by his mouth but still covered by her hands. Nearly shaking too, he gripped those hands, and pulled them away. He barely stopped a moan from escaping his mouth as he took in the sight of her hardened nipples. He needed a taste.

"I'm going to take you long and slow, and all through the night. I'm going to pleasure us both, but don't ever forget why you're here. Your pleasure is mine. I own it."

Her gasp of arousal was his reward. As he pulled her down onto his lap, he knew that he was done playing. He needed her, and he needed her now.

CHAPTER TWELVE

J EWELL COULD TELL she was on the verge of an incredible orgasm. Blake had taken her mouth greedily while he ran his hands down her back and pulled her against his thick arousal. Her dance movements had made the little vibrating toy inside her keep changing position, and she was dripping with desire as she sat on his lap.

His kiss took her breath away and made her body ache. Yes, she was doing this because she'd been forced into it, but it wasn't turning out to be a hardship. If she was going to give up her virginity, she had a feeling that this man was a good person to lose it to.

He made her burn, made her want him with nothing but a look from his smoldering eyes. He was cynical and demanding, but he was passionate and strong, and she couldn't pretend she didn't want to bring this song and dance they were doing to its foregone conclusion.

His mouth left hers, allowing her to take in a needed breath of air — not that it stayed long in her lungs. He moved to her breasts, and as he sucked one pebbled nipple before nipping it gently, she tried to gulp in oxygen, but found that she just couldn't do it.

When he shifted to the other side, and licked the sensitive bud at the same time as he ground his hips against her swollen core, she quit trying to hold back the pleasure that was consuming her. Her muscles tensed, and she cried out as she felt the pure bliss of release.

As she quivered in his arms, he sucked harder on her nipple, drawing out her orgasm to what felt like infinity. When it was over, she sagged forward against his chest, too weak even to move and thankful that his arms were holding her up. Sleep beckoned to her.

"We aren't done, Jewell," he whispered, his breath fanning her neck.

"I...I...can't do any...more."

"Oh, Jewell, you can and you *will*. You've been pleasured all day — I've watched you come over and over again. Now it's my turn. Now *you* get to please *me*."

It seemed impossible to her, but the deep timbre of his voice began awakening her body once more. There was no way she could survive this. A normal human being surely had to have a cap on how much physical pleasure he or she could receive in a single day.

"Please, Blake, please..."

"What are you begging for, Jewell?"

His hand drifted up and down her back, almost tenderly, as he asked her the question, and he grazed her neck tantalizingly with his lips.

"I...I don't know. I just...I don't think I can do anything more. It's too much, all of it too much." She hoped he'd have some kindness within him. She'd done everything he'd asked of her so far, and she was now overwhelmed.

"Let's see if I can change your mind."

He moved her to make her sit sideways on his lap; one of his arms cradled her as she rested her head against his chest. Then he stood up, slowly and smoothly, with her in his arms. She didn't have the energy even to protest — not that she would have. He wouldn't have allowed it.

He carried her through the apartment, to the stairs, up them, and into her room. Maybe he was going to let her sleep. Maybe they would continue this later, and maybe she would just gain back her energy, then run away as fast as she could before she grew too dependent on what he was giving her.

When he laid her down on the bed, she barely managed to open her eyes and look at him towering above her. But when he began removing his clothes, her stomach tightened and she directed her gaze downward. She wanted to see him again, wanted to look at his impressive manhood.

Then she *was* looking. At his long, thick, smooth staff, hard, ready to plunge inside her. His size made fear and desire do battle within her. She was glad he'd made her insert the toy. Her initial thought about it — that it might help stretch her — had been silly and naïve, because the toy was nothing compared to him. But it certainly made her wet, made her folds more eager to hold him.

The tip of his shaft gleamed with his desire, making her grow even wetter, and she was amazingly wet already. Yes, she was tired, and she felt as if she couldn't go on. But oh how she wanted him, wanted to feel what it was like to be taken by a virile man like Blake.

"Are you ready for me, Jewell? Are you ready to quit coming on your own? If you thought you felt good with your previous orgasms today, it won't hold a candle to what I am going to give you." He sat on the bed caressing her thighs as he spread her legs wide open.

"I…I'm afraid." She was so mortified to admit that.

He stopped touching her and looked at her with suspicion. "Why would you be afraid?"

She tensed, not willing to tell him the truth. "You're…um…large…" That was the truth, if not quite the whole truth. He was indeed large.

He laughed as he resumed rubbing her. "You must have been with pathetic men before me."

She refused to respond to that statement. She couldn't have spoken even if she'd wanted to, because he leaned over her and ran his tongue along her stomach before moving downward and kissing her thighs.

Spreading her legs as far as he could, Blake again found her pulsing little bundle of nerves and sucked on it and licked it while his fingers slid slowly inside her, then he got hold of the toy inside and began pulling it.

She shook with ecstasy mixed with a shot of pain as the toy moved inside her heat. Then she felt her body release the foreign object. She wanted to squeeze her thighs shut in relief. Pleasure was a good thing, she was discovering, but a woman could take only so much before she could no longer move.

"Ah, Jewell, you are so wet, so hot, so ready for me," Blake growled before swiping his tongue up and down her folds.

"Yes, oh yes," she gasped as her head twisted on the pillow. She was ready for him, ready for it all. Her fear was evaporating quickly, and she wasn't worried about pain, because at this moment she felt it would be more painful not to have him inside her.

He moved away and she heard the crinkling of a packet, telling her he was protecting them both, and then he was climbing up the bed, covering her body with his. Now he was right there, right in position, his face lined up with hers, his arousal pressing against her heat.

"Open your eyes, Jewell. I want to see what you're feeling when I'm buried deep inside of you."

"No." It was the first time she'd refused him, outright told him no. But she didn't want him to see her expression, didn't want to share that intimacy with him. She couldn't handle that.

"Open your eyes, Jewell — now!" he commanded, the head of his desire pressing into her.

Oh my, it felt good. The feel of his thick, hot shaft was so much better than the cold, lifeless toy that had been inside her all day.

"Nooo," she groaned as she lifted her hips, hoping to push him into entering her, hoping he would lose control before he could get her to open her eyes.

"Now, Jewel! Open them now!" He leaned down and bit her lower lip, sending a burst of pain through her, causing her eyes to pop open in surprise.

He smiled as he got what he wanted, and before she could even think about closing her eyes again, he drove his hips forward, filling her with one powerful thrust.

Before she could even think about stopping it, a cry of pain shot from her mouth as her body tensed. That had been nothing like what she'd been expecting, and she wanted to back away, wanted to push him from her. It was too much, way too much. It hurt, it was foreign, it was just too much.

"What in the hell?"

Blake froze, his eyes wide as he gazed down into her face. Myriad emotions passed through his eyes — confusion, anger, surprise, desire...

"Speak now, and speak fast, Jewell."

She couldn't do this. She'd been wrong. Yes, desire had

overcome her, her body had burned, and, despite everything, she still wanted him. But she couldn't do this. It was too much — too intimate, too consuming, too much!

She turned her head away so she wouldn't grow weak and look at him. She was barely holding her tears at bay, and she wanted only to escape. She knew struggling would be useless, so she lay there stiffly beneath him, his body still connected to hers in the most intimate way possible.

"Talk to me now!"

His angry shout startled her into turning back to look at him. Fury was brewing in his eyes.

"I...I can't," she said, her lip beginning to tremble.

"This is a trick. It has to be a trick." He now sounded as if he were the one begging.

"No. No. This is just wrong. We shouldn't do this. This is wrong." She needed to get away from him, but she was still held prisoner by his body.

"How in the hell can you be a virgin? You work at a whorehouse." He'd lowered his voice, but his words hurt far more than his shouting did.

"Yes, I'm a whore," she said quietly. And she was — she knew she was. She had agreed to sell her body. There was no other word for what she was. Her reasons didn't matter.

"It's not possible."

"Obviously it is. Are you going to finish this or let me go?" Jewell was almost surprised by her words, but she couldn't continue speaking to him while he remained within her body.

The pain had gone away, and now the fullness of him, the pressure against her inner core, was making her again feel those pangs of arousal. She didn't want that anymore.

When he shifted and his chest brushed against her, her nipples throbbed, and he suddenly seemed to notice as she wriggled beneath him, trying to make the desire go away.

He withdrew only a few inches from her, then slid easily back in, her slick heat beckoning to him.

"Don't get any ideas in your head about this turning into a relationship. The second that you don't please me, the second you don't give to me everything I want, our time is finished. Do you understand that?"

She knew he could see the fear on her face, but she couldn't speak, couldn't unmuddle her thoughts. However she also knew she didn't want to be with him forever, and didn't want to fall in love with him. He had nothing to worry about on that score. Then she grew angry, and fire lit up her eyes. She squared her shoulders and now refused to look away from the matching flare in his intense eyes.

"I expect the same from you. I want your money. You want my body. I think we understand each other just fine."

She could see rage consume Blake at her words. Though he'd made it abundantly clear that he thought all women were out to get whatever they could, what she'd just said seemed to be a slap in his face for some unfathomable reason.

"I'll make you forget all about money," he said, gripping the back of her neck less than gently, he surged within her, making her cry out in pleasure. No pain was anywhere to be found.

"Not possible." Afraid of him as she was, she never would back down from him.

Or so she thought for a brief moment. When his mouth connected with hers, she knew the battle was ending.

"Virgin or not, money or not, you want me, Jewell," he growled. "And now you're mine." He began moving slowly in and out of her, making her core burn with need, making her body tremble beneath him, and making her climb toward another release, this one low in her stomach, building stronger and stronger, stronger than anything she'd felt all day long.

"I hate you for this," she said, panting.

"I don't care," he replied coolly. He brought his head down and stopped all words with a kiss that stole her every thought away.

He now moved faster, his manhood rubbing her in every pleasurable way possible, his lips caressing hers and consuming her cries. The faster he moved, the higher her pleasure grew, and the more her sense of guilt vanished.

When his body tensed and he groaned heavily, she knew they were nearing the end.

"I'm going to come, Jewell. I'm going to shoot deep inside you. Come with me." Grabbing her hair, he held her in place and took her lips with an urgency that inflamed her.

A passionate scream was ripped from her as he slammed against her, burying himself deep within her core, setting her release free, and making her body convulse with the overload of sensation. He'd been right. The sexual pleasure she'd felt during the day was nothing, nothing at all, compared to what she felt right now.

He almost shouted in ecstasy as he shook within her, as his thick desire pulsed powerfully against her walls. His release went on for what seemed like forever, and then he collapsed against her, his body weight molding her into the bed.

Too spent to move, Jewell shut her eyes. It was all too much, and there was no possible way she could continue this way. Sleep gave her the only relief she could feel while she was with Blake. Sleep was her sanctuary.

CHAPTER THIRTEEN

BLAKE TURNED TO the side as Jewell's body relaxed beneath him. He knew she'd fallen asleep. He felt the urge to shake her, to wake her up. How dare she not tell him she was a virgin? Had she really believed that he wouldn't realize that? Had she wanted to hide it from him?

He was in no way interested in spending more than a few nights with this woman, so whether she was a virgin or not didn't matter to him. She was still selling herself, and though he might be her first lover, he certainly wouldn't be her last. He would take her back to Relinquish Control on Sunday, as planned, and she would move on to the next man.

And Blake had no doubt that she'd be chosen again soon. Jewell had a lot going for her — that odd innocence shining in her eyes, an eagerness to please, and yet still a stubbornness to prove that she would never be fully owned. She would be chosen over and over again, until the day a man took that look away from her.

He certainly didn't want to be the man who did that. Wait!

What the hell? Anger rushed through him at that sudden thought. He absolutely refused to have any sympathy for this woman. She had lied to him already, had played games with him since the moment their eyes had connected.

Disentangling himself from her, he stood, then felt his stomach tighten when she whimpered in her sleep and reached for him. He wanted to crawl back into her bed, to pull her close to him.

No. He couldn't do that!

Carefully, so as not to wake her, he covered her naked body, walked from her room, and went straight into his bathroom. He stood beneath the shower spray for a long time, as if it would wash her from his system.

It didn't work.

Half an hour later, wearing only a towel, he found himself standing next to her bed again and watching her as she slept, her face so young, her lips turned up in the smallest of smiles, her breathing deep and even.

"I'm only about to do this because I want her near me when I feel the urge to take her. It's all about convenience." He said the words aloud, though not loudly, but he knew he was lying to himself. Still, he couldn't stop from reaching for her, from pulling her sleeping body into his arms and from enjoying how it felt to have her head rest trustingly against his chest as he carried her carefully toward his own room.

No woman had ever slept in his bed. Ever. He'd never allowed something so intimate. Yet when he laid her down on his massive mattress and watched as she snuggled into the pillow, her smile growing just a little bit bigger, he felt the first stirrings of peace he'd felt in a long time — maybe ever.

Refusing to analyze that, because he knew that if he did, he wouldn't be able to let this situation continue, Blake crawled into the bed beside her. He pulled her against him and nearly came undone when she sought him out even in sleep, pressing even closer to him.

His body hardened and he thought about flipping her on her back and waking her up by plunging deep inside her heat. That's why he'd brought her to his bed, wasn't it? Of course it was. So he should do that without a second thought.

He still didn't make a move on her. He just continued to hold her, involuntarily caressing her back with his hands. Tomorrow he'd surely be himself again. This out-of-character behavior had to be from the shock of discovering her innocence. That's all it was. It simply couldn't be that he actually cared about this woman. He would never care about any woman.

Certainly, he was only holding back from having sex with her again because she was a virgin, and he knew she'd be sore. He didn't want to make it worse. He needed to give her a few hours to heal so she could be a better lover to him for the rest of the week she owed him.

Even though he was lying to himself again, Blake felt better. He'd expected that sleep would take hours — days even — to come to him, but it wasn't long before he joined her in an untroubled slumber.

CHAPTER FOURTEEN

HOW IN THE hell did I end up with a virgin from a damn escort service?"

Blake had been ranting as he paced back and forth in his brother's living room. He threw back a burning shot of scotch before moving to the window to look out at the picturesque view of the boats gliding effortlessly across the busy inlet.

"I think it's funny as hell. You're the only guy I know who goes to a place like Relinquish Control and picks the most innocent girl there. Whatever gets your rocks off, I guess," Tyler said as he leaned back lazily on his sofa.

"Shut up! I don't even know why I went to the stupid place, but I did, and she ended up at my house. Now I have to figure out what the hell to do."

"Did she please you?" Tyler asked.

Blake turned and crossed over to the chair facing his brother. "The sex was out of this world, and though she has a temper, she listens, which is a must. Of course, if she were a complete doormat, what fun would that be?"

"It's all about the sex, so who cares what she was before you met her?"

"Yeah, but a virgin? I want nothing to do with that."

"Well, she isn't a virgin anymore."

That made Blake stop. "I guess you're right. What good would it do me to send her back? It's not like she didn't know what she was getting into. She put her body up for sale. You know, though, she's not as greedy as she might be — or maybe she was just a bit stupid. Had she told McKenzie what she was, the woman could have gotten a lot more for her. Some men get off on that sort of thing."

"But not you?" Tyler said with a chuckle.

"Go to hell, Tyler. You and I both know we aren't ever going to settle down, and when we're with women, we sure as hell want them to know what they're doing in the sack, because that's pretty much the only place we waste time with them."

"So you aren't really happy with her? Then send her back."

"I didn't say I wasn't happy with her. I just said that I didn't want the responsibility of a damn virgin," Blake said, getting more and more frustrated.

"Okay, but it's too late now, so either suck it up and finish out your week or send her packing, but whichever you choose, please quit acting like a love-struck fool."

"You're a freaking pain in the ass!" Blake thundered.

"Yeah, I've heard that about fifty thousand times since I was a child," Tyler said with another chuckle, but the mirth faded from his expression and he looked solemnly at his brother.

Blake didn't want the conversation to turn. He knew where it was headed, and it terrified him. Not much struck Blake with fear these days, but the topic they were about to embark on was the one thing that could bring him to his knees.

"Sunday is the day," Tyler said quietly.

"I know. But we have to think of other things. It's been twenty-five years, Tyler. Don't you think we've allowed that woman to punish us long enough?" Blake said dryly.

"It's easier for you to hide it, to push it from your mind, but I also know you never would have gone to a place like Relinquish Control if it weren't the twenty-fifth anniversary of their death."

"Yeah. I know. This is a tough year, but I think we need to get over it. We've suffered enough, and that sadistic bitch can rot in hell for all eternity."

"I don't disagree with you, but are we going to do anything to mark the date? The nightmares have come back, and I can't...I..." Tyler trailed off as a shudder passed through him.

"I haven't had nightmares for years. I've been waiting for them to return, but nothing has happened so far. What does Byron want to do?"

"He said that he wanted to do absolutely nothing, that he doesn't ever think about them."

"He's full of crap. We'll go to their graves. We're going to let this go once and for all," Blake said fiercely.

"How? Yes, you can say that, but years of therapy didn't come close to erasing it, Blake. We watched our parents get murdered in front of us," Tyler said, his voice rising.

"And that happened because our mother was such a selfish bitch that she didn't care if our father's death traumatized us, her own freaking children. Her game backfired and we got to pay the price!"

Blake couldn't talk about that time in his life, that long night twenty-five years ago, without overwhelming anger. But he wouldn't take out his rage on Tyler. They had done that to each other for years. It was over.

"Byron will come. We'll let this go and never speak of it again."

Tyler's eyes narrowed. "Is that an order?"

"Come on, Tyler! You know it's not that way with us. You're just itching to fight. Our sanity — yours, mine, and Byron's — depends on our getting past this."

"If you're letting it go so well, then explain this escort person you hired."

"I don't know what in the hell is going on with Jewell. Call it temporary weakness, but that weakness just ended." Blake had a look of grim determination. "I will use her for sex and then easily ship her off after the week is over."

"We'll see," Tyler said with a smirk that made Blake want to crush his brother against a wall with a bulldozer.

"Look. I don't need this woman for anything more than sex. So what if she hasn't been with another man before me? I don't give a damn. She'll certainly be with a lot of men after me, a lot of men paying good money for her."

"That is probably the only truth you've spoken about her... and yourself," Tyler said. He sounded as if he didn't have a care in the world.

"Thanks for all the helpful words of advice, little brother," Blake snapped.

Tyler's grin widened. "You know I'll be there for you anytime."

Blake didn't bother to respond. He didn't know why he'd come to Tyler, why he'd felt the need to share, but it seemed that whenever the brothers had a problem, they always ended up on each other's doorsteps. It would be that way for life.

He left Tyler's house, got into his car, and made his way to the office building. Work was good. It was what he needed. He wouldn't think about his parents, wouldn't think about Jewell Weston, wouldn't think about any of it. He would clear his mind and focus on numbers.

It's what he'd done in the past, and it had always worked. Why in the hell wasn't it working now?

CHAPTER FIFTEEN

THE SMELL OF musk and spice drifted pleasantly across the pillow and into Jewell's sleep-fogged brain. She inhaled, wondering where she'd smelled that before.

Then her eyes flew open and she twisted her head to look around, her body stiffening until she realized she was alone. The night before came flooding back to her, and her face flushed when she realized what she'd done.

Okay, she'd known she was going to "do it," and it had been out-of-this-world great, but she wasn't supposed to feel that way. She was supposed to be doing this for one reason, and that reason wasn't for herself.

Still, she couldn't keep her eyes from closing in soft remembrance as she thought back over last night. After falling asleep, or, more accurately, passing out, she hadn't even noticed when Blake had carried her to another bed. Sometime in the night, she'd woken to find his head buried between her sore thighs and it hadn't taken him long to send her spiraling into another mind-blowing orgasm.

When he then moved up the bed and brushed her lips with his incredibly hard arousal, she hadn't hesitated to open to him. She'd taken his velvet skin into her mouth and sucked him until he'd released his pleasure onto her greedy tongue.

They hadn't spoken, hadn't acknowledged the power of their night. He'd simply pulled her back into his arms and she'd fallen blissfully back asleep. Now, as she sat up in what had to be his bed, she wondered what was happening. Hadn't he told her when she'd first arrived that she wasn't allowed in his room?

She had no idea what she was supposed to do next. This short time with Blake Knight was a constant up and down, and yet she wasn't miserable being with him. Was it because he kept throwing her so off balance?

She had five more nights with him. After that, she'd go back to Relinquish Control, and the muddle her brain had become would get straightened out. That was good. It was what she needed.

Finally getting up, she walked to his bathroom and gasped at the large sunken tub and a glass-enclosed shower big enough for at least six people. Oh, her mouth watered at even the thought of using either one, but she didn't want to risk his wrath. Granted, he'd brought her into his bedroom himself, but she was sure he'd want her to leave right away and not take advantage of the super-fancy facilities there.

Grabbing a thick robe she found hanging on the wall, she wrapped her petite body in it and returned to his bedroom. She cracked the door to the hall open and looked both ways. No one else had been in his apartment the day before, but that didn't mean there wouldn't be someone today, and she really didn't want to meet anyone for the first time while doing the walk of shame from Blake's room in his too-big bathrobe.

The coast was clear, so she snuck down the hall, entered her own temporary room, and headed straight to her bathroom. Climbing into her shower — it was large, but nothing like Blake's — she stood beneath the hot spray for several minutes without moving, welcoming the relief to her stiff muscles.

She had used muscles she didn't even know existed last night, and she suspected she would continue to be sore for a few days. That was a real bummer. After all, she'd be with Blake for the next five days, and he probably wasn't going to give her much time to rest.

Though she would power her way through it, she may go searching for a hot tub. A place this large and grand would have to have one, wouldn't it? If not, she'd soak for hours in the tub in her bathroom. She wouldn't be very good to him later that night if she couldn't even bend.

When she felt a bit better, she turned off the shower and went back into her room. That's when she noticed a bag sitting on her bed. Damn! No doubt Blake wanted her to wear some skimpy little outfit again for his own pleasure while he checked in on her any time he wanted with his house cameras.

Maybe if she didn't open the bag, she could pretend ignorance. That sounded liked a fantastic idea to her. So she walked to her large closet and dressed in the most comfortable clothes she could find — though she'd hardly call them comfortable. The shorts barely covered her behind, and the sheer top showed a lot more than it hid, but at least she wouldn't get overheated. That was always a bonus.

When she reached the kitchen and found her phone on the counter, several messages showed on the screen. Could she pretend she hadn't seen them as well? As a new message beeped in, she knew that wasn't going to be possible.

So she picked it up reluctantly, unlocked the screen, and opened her inbox.

> You appeared to sleep well. Make sure you are
> well rested for tonight.
>
> I want you to take a long soak in the tub in my
> room. I've had special bath salts delivered that
> will help ease your soreness. Spend at least an
> hour in the hot water.
>
> Don't pretend you didn't see the bag. Go back up
> there and open it.

Before she could even think about which message to respond to first, another one popped up on her screen. This one made her smile and then frown.

> Yes, I am watching you. Good morning, Jewell.
> You did well last night. We will discuss it at length
> later.

She looked up along the walls, trying to discover where the cameras were located. If she could somehow find them, maybe she could find some places in his home where she could hide. She so craved some semblance of privacy.

Did he have cameras in his bathroom, too? Would he watch her as she bathed? Just the thought caused her stomach to stir. Blake seemed to have awakened something inside her, and she didn't know whether she'd be able to turn it back off. That was a terrifying thought, because this was absolutely temporary.

And still, even though Blake wasn't Mr. Perfect, and he was demanding and curt, he also didn't seem to be the type to do really sick things. What if the next guy wasn't so easy? What if the lifestyle he was into was something she just couldn't do? She couldn't get past the words some of the other girls had spoken.

They'd talked about how men liked to whip them, make

them bow down at their feet, feed them from a bowl on the floor. There were other things, sex things, that made her gag just to think of them. She couldn't do such things. Or could she? Hadn't she vowed to do anything for her brother? But would he want her to sink so low? Would he do the same for her? Of course he would, at least if he were older.

She just prayed she would never be forced into choosing between her brother and her pride. Because if she were treated in such a demeaning way, it might well not matter whether she saved her brother or not, because she would be lost forever.

> **Answer me, Jewell. Now!**
>
> *Oh, you are impatient, Mr. Knight. I was just trying to decide what to answer first.*
>
> **I don't like waiting for anyone.**
>
> *Then you will surely be disappointed a lot in your lifetime.*

Not knowing why she was doing it, Jewell added a bit of salt to her comment by looking up at the walls with a mocking smile. She might not know where the cameras were, but she certainly hoped he got the message. She felt a whole heck of a lot braver when she was communicating with Blake by text message and not in person. He wasn't quite so intimidating.

> *You really need a good spanking. You're not jumping when I say jump.*
>
> *You didn't tell me how high.*

Instead of striking terror into her, his threat gave her a shiver of excitement. She didn't know this man, and had no idea what he was capable of, but if he wanted to really hurt her, wouldn't he have shown that already? She hadn't seen anything so far in his place that looked menacing, and she had spent the entire day wandering the apartment, so she would have turned up something if it were there.

> You're pushing me, Jewell…

> *Maybe you need to be pushed. Maybe too many people kiss your ass and that makes you a grumpy man.*

When there was no response to her last message, Jewell wondered whether she'd taken things too far, just like the last time they engaged in a phone war. Although texting a message made her feel braver, she didn't want him to send her away, didn't want to lose the money future jobs would give her, the money to get her own apartment, the money that would show the judge she would be a fit guardian for her brother. She was again close to apologizing when a message finally came through.

> Go take your bath, Jewell. Now! I will show you later what happens when someone displeases me.

This time she didn't reply. Pacing worriedly from the living room to the kitchen and back again, she chewed on her thumbnail. Was he serious?

> I can see you are wising up, Jewell. Don't try to challenge me. You will lose.

Relief flooded through her at seeing his message. True, it was another order, and it wasn't a very pleasant one, but he wasn't telling her she'd have to leave. He wasn't screaming at her with exclamation marks galore or in all capital letters. Why she felt the need to challenge him she didn't know, but as much as she was trying to suppress her personality to get through this week, she couldn't kill it completely.

She'd been raised by a strong, beautiful, brilliant mother, and she respected herself. Sure, she didn't always make the best choices, but couldn't that be said about everyone? She was still a good person and she still deserved to be treated with respect, even if she had agreed to work for an agency with the name Relinquish Control.

Even if she *was* selling her body.

With an extra sway in her hips, she turned and moved toward the stairs. Hadn't she told herself she wanted to use his bath anyway? Of course she had. So even though he was ordering her to take a bath, it was no skin off her...back. Let him think he'd won some imaginary skirmish in their battle of wills.

She went first to her room and looked at the bag on her bed. She didn't want to open it, but she also didn't want to keep challenging this man. So she picked up the bag and looked inside, then really hoped he was decent enough not to have a camera in her room — but she knew, oh yes, she knew, that he did. Of course the bag contained more lingerie, in a style that would show everything to him. And of course it would make her feel like the slut he wanted her to be.

Angry tears sprang into her eyes, but she refused to acknowledge them herself or lift her face so he could see them. If she didn't show that she cared, he couldn't be satisfied by his stupid little games. Once the tears went away, she looked up with another smirk and moved toward his bedroom.

Once back in his large bathroom, she walked to the tub and started the water. He doubtless had a camera pointing right at her here. Good! She hoped he suffered while he was at his stiff desk with his tight pants. Because she was ticked off now, and she was more than happy to put on one hell of a show for Blake Knight.

She took off her clothes slowly, letting them fall to the floor in a nice little heap, then went over to the vanity mirror and lifted her arms, pulled up her hair and placed it in a bun. At least the man thought of everything, having far more vanity products available to her than she had owned in her last apartment. She ran her hands down her neck and over her breasts, then down her stomach.

Her phone was sitting on the counter and it immediately beeped, but she ignored it. Instead she sashayed over to the tub and picked up the jar of the bath salts he'd demanded that she use. As she bent over to spread them on the top of the water, she hoped he got a really good view.

When her phone beeped again, she looked toward the ceiling and shook her head with a smile. He'd told her to take a bath and that's exactly what she was going to do. The phone went off three more times, and with a frustrated breath, she went over and picked it up with the intention of turning it off. However, she would just check the messages first.

> You don't like your garments? I picked them out personally.

> Don't ignore your phone. I've already told you I don't like that. I shouldn't have to repeat myself.

> Dammit, Jewell, quit being difficult. Do you want

this to end? I'm more than willing to go and find a
woman who is more cooperative.

That one made her stomach clench, but she couldn't show
that to him, couldn't give him such power. He thought she was
nothing more than a slut, and she had to agree with him there,
but she couldn't fully let go of her pride. Still, she needed to
make him happy.

Is that little striptease for me? You're redeeming
yourself.

Turn off your phone now, Jewell, and enjoy your
bath. I'll be watching…

Watch away, Mr. Knight.

With that message sent, she clicked off her phone and
walked to the tub. If he wanted a show, he was soon going to
find that her earlier performance had merely been a teaser for
the main event.

CHAPTER SIXTEEN

B LAKE LOOSENED HIS tie. He knew he should turn off the monitors and stop watching. He knew exactly what Jewell was doing. She was trying to gain back some of the control that she felt he was taking away. Okay, the control that he was definitely taking away.

Instead of being frustrated with her, instead of wanting to punish her, to send her away, he was more excited than he'd been when he first met her. If she were refusing his orders outright, he wouldn't be able to tolerate it, but she wasn't pushing it that far.

No. She was pushing him just enough to turn him on, to make him want to leave work and rush home so he could show her who was in charge. He would take great pleasure in doing just that.

He had to force himself to stay seated. He refused to rush home, because that *was* giving her too much power and he wasn't willing to do that. No, this exciting battle of wills would continue, and he was going to sit right where he was.

And as much as he told himself he ought to focus on

anything other than Jewell and the clear water in the tub, he still found himself fixated on her…and the show she was putting on was making his office feel a whole hell of a lot hotter.

When Jewell slipped down into the water, the sway of her breasts mesmerized him. She grabbed a bottle from the side of the tub and squirted a good amount of soap into her hands, then rubbed them together before starting at her neck and then brushing her hands down the sweet curve of her breasts.

When she began massaging her nipples with her thumb and forefinger, letting her head lean back against the rim of the tub, he felt his arousal pulse. This video feed lacked sound, and he was almost grateful for that fact, because when he saw her mouth open, he had no doubt a soft moan was escaping her sweet red lips, and the actual sound would probably hit him with cardiac arrest.

He could focus only on her as her hands next traveled down the luscious line of her stomach before her legs spread out in the large tub, and then she was rubbing along her hot, sleek folds and her mouth opened in a big O.

That was it.

So what if she had more power? He would certainly take it back. He darted up from his chair, flicked off the monitor, and walked from his office. No one on that floor said a word as he marched off to his private elevator.

Blake jumped into his car and peeled out of the parking garage with squealing tires before entering the busy roads and rushing to the freeway. He wanted to get home, and he wanted to get there fast. When he made it to his apartment complex, he was amazed he managed to park the car straight.

Jumping out, he dashed to his elevator and, once he got inside, tapped his foot impatiently while the stupid box took an obscene amount of time to reach his penthouse apartment.

He only slowed down when he was finally inside the apartment. That's where he took a deep breath and told himself that he was in control, that he could turn around and walk back out if he chose to. Yeah, right. If that were the case, why did his feet keep moving forward, and why was he now bounding up the stairs?

His bathroom door was cracked open, and he heard a sigh that made his already hard body throb painfully. After stripping naked, he took another breath, then flung the damned door open.

It banged against the wall, and his reward was seeing Jewell's eyes widen.

She sat up in shock. "What are you doing here?"

"You were putting on such a great show, I wanted to see it in person," he said as he strode forward, his arousal jutting out proudly.

"I...uh..."

"Don't know what to say now that I'm standing here, Jewell? Did you really think you could play games with me and not see them through?"

He stepped down into the tub before she could answer, and he pulled her onto his lap, his body thanking him when her skin came into contact with his.

"I just hate the cameras," she said before gasping as his mouth took a nipple and sucked it hard.

"Well, I happen to love them," he told her before switching sides, and making a low moan tumble from her throat. "And I'm taking you now."

He drew her up onto his erection, and then pulled her down, giving a rumble of pleasure as he filled her tight heat.

"Damn, you feel good," he groaned as he began lifting her up and down on him.

He didn't let her speak as he kept up the primitive rhythm. He just grabbed the back of her neck and his lips claimed hers. The sweet taste of her mouth and the feel of her inner walls gripping him tightly were quickly making him lose any vestige of control.

Finally, with a growl, he forced his hips up almost violently while pulling her down upon him, and then he exploded inside her. Her cries echoed off the bathroom walls as she found her own pleasure simultaneously.

It was several moments later when he realized he hadn't even thought about protection. Overcome with panic, he quickly pulled her off him and moved away.

"What's wrong?" She scooted back farther, lifting her arms up in a protective gesture.

"I didn't use a condom," he said, his voice hoarse. The last thing he needed or wanted was a child.

"I'm...uh...I'm on birth control. It was the first thing they did at the...um...employment agency," she stuttered, and relief washed through him.

In his panic he'd forgotten what McKenzie had told him — the girls were protected both from pregnancy *and* tested for disease each time they returned from a client. Still, he didn't trust birth control. He always made sure he was protected — without fail.

"It won't happen again." He stood up and stepped from the tub, his desire sated, and the scare of an unplanned pregnancy eliminating, for now at least, the need to take her back to his bed for another bout. "I'm going back to work."

He walked from the bathroom; his emotions were turbulent as he got dressed and left his bedroom. He was grateful she waited to emerge until he was finished. This woman had made him leave work in the middle of the day, had made him forget condoms, had made him want and do things he never had before.

Maybe he *should* send her back after all — job paid in full. That would be much safer for his sanity. But even as he rode back down to the parking garage, he knew that wasn't going to happen.

He wasn't nearly finished with Jewell Weston. Just a few more days with her would do the trick. Ignoring the pang that idea caused, he focused now on anything but her. Instead of driving back to his offices, he decided to head to the work site of a large mall his company was building.

What he needed right now was a hammer and nails so he could pound out his frustration on inanimate objects. He sure as hell hoped he didn't run into either of his brothers, because there was no way he could explain his black mood or the chaos now ruling his thoughts.

CHAPTER SEVENTEEN

J EWELL HAD KNOWN she was innocent about the ways of the world, and even about human nature — but downright stupid, too? Why had she felt the need to put on that show for Blake? How could she not have realized there would be consequences? She should just be his perfect little servant for the next few days, and then go back to her place of "employment" and forget all about the man.

Apparently she really *had* needed more training. Until now, she hadn't understood why Ms. Beaumont normally had the girls train for so long. But Jewell couldn't believe it would have worked in her case. You had to have your soul broken and rebuilt with their so-called training. And she couldn't imagine never being able to think for herself. But unlike most of the girls there, she had no intention of staying for long, despite the outrageous sums of money involved.

She knew her own worth, and knew that an escort service wasn't where she belonged. So if she did just roll over and become the submissive little woman that Blake wanted, wouldn't that forever change her? Wouldn't that make her less of a person? Right now, she was a mass of confusion.

No matter how much she thought about it, the answers wouldn't come to her. She had to get dressed and get out of his apartment for a while. She just needed a walk — that was all. A breath of fresh air, so to speak. It was past time for Jewell to get the heck out of the apartment. She couldn't stand the stuffy place for even one second longer.

As she opened the front door, she was stopped short by a giant of a man who was holding a key out, about to insert it into the lock.

"You must be Jewell," the man said, and she drew back a step, then her eyes narrowed and she took a good look at his face.

She knew that face. She'd seen it a dozen times as she'd passed by the picture on Blake's wall. It was one of his brothers. Though Blake was a tall man, his brother had a few inches on him. She didn't know which one he was.

"Tyler Knight," he said, holding out his hand when she still said nothing, leaving an awkward silence between them.

She finally found her voice and accepted the hand that was hanging in midair, waiting for her decision. "Jewell Weston." What would be the point in lying about her name? He already knew who she was.

"So you're the girl scrambling my brother's brain this week," he said with a laugh after releasing her hand.

"I wouldn't say I'm scrambling his brain. He's a tough egg to crack," she said, being careful not to say too much. This was Blake's brother, after all.

"Ah, Jewell, you are most certainly scrambling his brain," Tyler told her before pulling her out the door and firmly shutting it behind him. "Where are you off to? I didn't think my brother would let you leave the apartment."

She wasn't sure whether he was serious or not, but he was

more right than he knew. Blake would probably be furious that she was leaving, but she had to get out of there for a while. She would just have to deal with the consequences later.

"I'm free to do what I want." She wasn't, but there was no way she was telling that to another living soul.

"Good. We'll go have lunch. I'm starving," he said, placing her arm through his.

That made her more than a little uncomfortable. "I was just going to go for a quick stroll. I don't want to be gone too long." Blake would be home by six and she couldn't be gone when he arrived.

"Nonsense. Everyone needs to eat, and I refuse to eat alone. You can fill me in on what you're doing to my brother." He didn't give her an out; she had to go with him.

When they reached the outside of the building, Tyler was still holding on to her and pulling her along with him. Once again, her options were limited — she had the choice of following him or falling on her face if she stopped and he didn't.

"Are all three of you bossy and used to getting your way?"

Tyler kept on walking, but he laughed and threw her a nice smile. "Pretty much. What would you like to eat?"

"I'm easy," she said before wincing. Yeah, she was pretty damn easy. At least now she was. Talk about a depressing thought.

"All righty. Then sushi it is," he said as he approached a shiny black sports car — did all three brothers go for the same type of ride? — and held the passenger door open.

"Perfect." Raw fish didn't exactly float her boat, but maybe some company wouldn't be so bad.

Once Jewell had settled into her seat, Tyler rushed over to the driver's side and hopped in, then revved the engine and pulled out into traffic.

"So, is Blake treating you well?"

She didn't know how to answer that question. Had Blake sent his brother to quiz her? Was Tyler going to report all her answers? She had to be very careful.

"I can't complain. You know this isn't a relationship, right?"

"Any time a man and woman are together, it's a relationship, babe. Don't fool yourself." He turned and winked at her, nearly giving her a heart attack when the car swerved a bit across the centerline.

"Well, I'll only be with him a few more days." She wasn't going to say he'd picked her up at an escort service, but she didn't want Tyler to think that they were going to bond and she was going to be around for a while.

"I'm not so sure about that," he said with a secret smile that seemed to say he knew a lot more than she did. She wished he would fill her in on what he did know.

When they drove up to a small restaurant, she jumped when her door opened unexpectedly. An attendant in uniform held out a hand to assist her. Then Tyler came around, took her arm again after tipping the attendant, and led her inside.

"I've been craving some fresh crab rolls," he said as he led her to the sushi bar and held out a seat for her before seating himself.

Jewell soon found herself relaxing as they were served, and Tyler began filling her in on old stories from the workplace, from a time when both he and Blake were more hands-on in their business.

"Yeah, I totally thought I was badass. Our electrician was nowhere to be found, and the lights were off, so I thought, how hard could it be to hook two wires together? We needed some light. I was up on the lift and, thinking the power was cut, grabbed the wrong wire. It sent me right down on my ass and scared the hell out of me. I don't frighten easily, but I walked from the building and went and laid down in the back of my truck for the next hour, thanking anyone up above who was listening that the electric jolt hadn't just stopped my heart."

"That is horrible," Jewell gasped. "Why didn't you go to the doctor?"

"Because I didn't get hurt. Yeah, my heart was beating erratically for a while, but I was fine. You can't run to the doctor for every little thing." He shrugged and popped a roll into his mouth.

"When it comes to electricity, I wouldn't mess around."

"Ha! Blake has done even worse. He was on the job site and his finger got caught in the door. Blood was pouring out, and all of a sudden he went all white, passed out, and smacked his head. Then, when he came to, he just wrapped his finger in tape and finished the day. It was two days later when the finger wouldn't stop throbbing that he finally agreed to go to the doctor. Not only was it infected, but he'd broken it in two places and had to have surgery because it had already begun to heal wrong."

"I don't think that's brave, Tyler. I think it's foolish."

He laughed again. "I dare you to tell him that."

"You have an infectious laugh," she said, and joined him. "And there's no way I'm telling him."

"You're just all talk, aren't you?" he said with a hint of sarcasm.

It soon became time to go and he led her back out to the car.

"Thank you for a great lunch, Tyler. I've enjoyed visiting with you. I really should get back, though." She'd begun to worry that Blake might be checking on her. She hadn't brought her cell phone, so he'd be furious if he'd been trying to get ahold of her.

"You are a buzzkill, Jewell, but I suppose I'll take you back now, so my brother doesn't think I'm trying to steal his woman." Tyler said, and threw the car into gear.

She didn't correct him. Why bother to repeat that she wasn't really his brother's woman? Whatever she was, it would be over in a few days.

A speaker in the car started ringing. She looked over to see what Tyler had done, but then she heard Blake's voice.

"I need you to get over to Bill's house," Blake told Tyler. "The stubborn fool sent our crew away. He said he wouldn't accept charity."

"What do you mean? I thought it was all taken care of," Tyler replied with a frown.

"Yeah. So did I. But when the roofing crew showed up, Bill came out and threatened to have the cops haul them off for trespassing. Tim called me and asked what to do. I told him to head out, that I would come talk to Bill. I got here thirty minutes ago and he said there was no way he would allow me to pay for him to get a new roof." Blake's frustrated sigh came through loud and clear over the speakers.

"Damned old man. There's no way that roof can last another winter. What are we gonna do?" Tyler asked as he turned on the freeway.

Jewell wasn't very familiar with the area, but it seemed to her they weren't moving toward Blake's apartment. Had Tyler forgotten she was in the car? She didn't want to say something and have Blake hear her, so she just fidgeted in her seat.

"It looks like we're roofing the place. He won't let us pay for it, but he sure as hell will let us climb up there and do it ourselves," Blake said, a smile clearly in his tone.

"Yeah, I can see that. What I can't see is you up there with your pristine white shirt, holding a hammer," Tyler joked.

"Whatever. I don't see you up on any roofs anymore either,"

Blake fired back.

"Point taken. Let's see if we still know how. I'm ten minutes out. See ya in a few." Tyler pushed a button and the call was disconnected.

Jewell sat there in silence a moment longer just to make sure Blake really was gone before she spoke. "Um, Tyler, I think you took a wrong turn," she finally said.

"Nope. Change of plans. We have to go roof a house." He turned off the freeway and headed down a city street.

"I...um...can't roof a building. Maybe you should just drop me off first," she said, growing more and more nervous as he continued in the same direction.

"No can do. We've already lost over half the day."

"I can't go there!" She was more insistent this time.

"Look, Jewell. Bill was my grandfather's best friend and has always been good to my brothers and I. He's also been the most stubborn old coot I've ever met in my life. He won't let us pay for anything for him, won't accept what he deems charity, but his roof needs fixing. The only way we're going to get it done is by doing it ourselves. And it's supposed to rain in a few days, so we have to haul ass. You'll be fine. You can visit with Bill while we work."

Tyler's tone seemed so reasonable, but she knew that Blake was going to flip out when he saw her pull up with his brother. He might be so furious that she'd gone to lunch with Tyler that he would call his driver and have her removed from his life right away.

Even though she would lose her job, the more time she spent with Blake, the more she realized that she most likely wouldn't be able to jump into this sort of thing again with another man. She just wasn't the sort of person who could keep selling her body. She'd just take her check, bank it, and then find any job at all. She wouldn't sleep until she'd turned up another opportunity. And really, there was no point in arguing with Tyler any further. The Knight men obviously didn't take no for an answer.

When they pulled up to a small home surrounded by at least two acres of land, and she saw Blake walking toward the car, her heart thundered. His eyes locked in on her in the passenger seat and his silver glare seared right through her, making her wish she were any other place in the world right then.

"Smile, Jewell," Tyler told her. "It looks like my brother is going to growl." He opened his door and said hello.

When Blake didn't reply to Tyler but instead went immediately to her side of the car and ripped open the door, she was seriously thinking of diving across the seat and out the driver's side door and making a run for it.

"What in the hell are you doing here?"

Words wouldn't come from her throat. When he took her arm and dragged her from the car, she shook in terror. This was going to be bad — really, really bad.

CHAPTER EIGHTEEN

A S HE BOXED Jewell in against the side of his brother's car, Blake couldn't remember ever being this angry. Ever. Fury rolled off of him in waves and he wanted to punish her, punish Tyler, punish anyone who dared to even look at him.

"Talk to me now, Jewell! Did you really think you could fuck me a few hours ago and then give it up to my brother?"

The fear in her eyes should please him. Let her fear him. It was smart of her. She wouldn't play any more games if she were afraid. When he was about to open his mouth again, though, he felt a hand on his shoulder flipping him around, and then pain shot through his jaw as the force of a punch sent him flying against the car right next to Jewell. She quickly scrambled away.

"What the hell?" Red flashed before Blake's eyes. He flung his head from side to side and lifted a hand, ready to pummel someone. But when he saw an answering rage in Tyler's normally easygoing face, he was startled enough to unclench his hand. "What was that for?" Blake asked, using his hand to rub his sore jaw.

"You're an asshole on the best of days, but you just insulted both me and Jewell with that asinine statement!" Tyler thundered.

"She's a prostitute. What else do you expect?" Blake snapped, and Tyler made another fist. This time, Blake was ready and sidestepped the hit, then gave his brother a baffled look. He didn't want to fight Tyler. He loved him. What was going on? He had to find out. "What in blazes has you so worked up, Tyler?"

"I stopped by your place and dragged Jewell out to lunch, then got your call. She's done nothing wrong and you're treating her worse than you'd treat a stranger you'd heard only bad things about. You can stay the hell away from her if you're going to abuse her with such offensive remarks."

"Um, do I need to run interference?"

Both men turned to see Byron standing there and looking back and forth between them with a brotherly smirk on his face.

"Stay out of this, Byron. I'm about to kick Blake's ass!"

"I would love to see the two of you go at it," Byron told them, "but Bill is standing in the doorway looking at you both like you've lost your minds. I think I agree with him."

"I certainly think *Tyler* has lost his mind. He slugged me," Blake said, keeping a wary eye on his brother.

"I'm sure you deserved it," Byron replied. "Now if you two girls can kiss and make up, we can actually get this show on the road." He stopped speaking when he finally noticed Jewell standing about ten feet away, looking in horror at the three brothers. "Ah! Now I see what's going on. It's always a woman..."

"I didn't do anything," Jewell said, surprising all three of them. "I basically got kidnapped and taken to lunch," she snapped before turning to Tyler. "Not that it didn't turn out to be a very nice lunch. Then Blake calls and I'm dragged here against my will, and the next thing I know punches are being thrown. If you want to act like Neanderthals, be my guest, but I want no part of it." She folded her arms across her chest.

Byron blinked. "Sooo, you're here with Tyler?"

"No, she's with me," Blake snapped. "Tyler decided he needed to 'bond' with her."

"Ah, a love triangle. That's a recipe for disaster," Byron said in a bored voice. "A foolproof one, so even my pitiful brothers couldn't screw it up."

"It is not a damn love triangle," Tyler snarled. "I can talk to a woman without the need to push her against a wall and take off all her clothes."

"All righty, then. Can we get to work now?" Byron asked.

"Yes!" both Tyler and Blake exclaimed.

"And what about me?" Jewell asked.

They all turned in her direction as if they'd completely forgotten she was even standing there.

"You can sit down and shut up," Blake told her.

To his utter surprise, her eyes narrowed and she stomped up to him, shoved her finger into his chest, and, after taking a deep breath, unleashed her wrath.

"I can put up with a lot, Blake Knight, and I have been doing just that over the past few days, but I am not going to have you talk to me like that in front of other people. I am a human being and I deserve at least a modicum of respect. Your brother forced me to come here, and I am not going to just sit around and wait. If you're all going to work, then I can do something, too."

No woman had ever snapped at him like this, or demanded his respect. He'd never before felt the urge to give in and do exactly what she was asking of him, either.

"No. It's too dangerous," he said, and thinking the subject was closed, he turned away.

"Then I'll find something to do on my own." She walked

toward Bill. "Hi. I'm Jewell. What can I do to help you?"

Blake stood there for several heartbeats as he watched Bill put out his hand, clasp hers, and give the first smile Blake had seen on the old man's face in years.

"Bill Berkshire. It's a pleasure to meet you, young lady. How about we start with a glass of iced tea, and then we'll find some work?"

"That sounds lovely." Jewell walked with Bill into the house after casting a final, contemptuous glance back at the boys.

Blake and his brothers were left standing there with their jaws hanging all the way down to the ground.

"Well, brother, that's a woman you might not want to let get away," Tyler said before he moved over to the work truck that Blake had one of his men deliver. He began putting on a tool belt.

After a moment, Blake shook his head and followed his brother. It was going to be a long day, and yes, he'd be having a talk with Jewell about her place in his life, but right now he just didn't have the time. She would definitely pay for her sins later, though.

Taking off his expensive suit jacket, he rolled up the sleeves of his white shirt before thinking twice and yanking it off, leaving him bare-chested. He was not dressed for this type of work, and in fact rarely swung a hammer these days. He was far beyond that. He only did it when he needed to work out his aggressions.

He'd already fiddled around one of the worksites today in hopes of dealing with the frustration he'd been feeling, but this job would cause a hell of a lot more sweat than what he'd been doing when his foreman had called and told him that Bill had sent the workmen away. He should curse the old man, but he knew he wouldn't.

The thought of getting revenge on Jewell kept him going as he climbed up onto Bill's roof during the hottest part of the day and ripped off the ridge cap, then began tearing down the shingles. Yes, revenge and swift punishment would most certainly be sweet.

CHAPTER NINETEEN

WHAT ARE YOU doing with a cad like Blake?" Jewell stopped sipping her glass of sweet iced tea and laughed. "I don't know, Bill, but I can tell you it's worth it. Because if I weren't with him, I never would have gotten to meet you. For that matter, what are *you* doing with a cad like Blake?" Her grin made Bill laugh in turn.

"I've known Blake since the day he was born," Bill said, and his smile began to disappear. "His father was a good man, but his mama beat the good right out of him — I mean Blake's dad. It broke the heart of my best friend, Blake's granddaddy. I was just glad he passed on before he saw the final chapter of their story play out."

"What do you mean?" She knew she shouldn't pry into Blake's life, but it was like watching a movie, one that you just couldn't turn off because you had to know how it ended.

"I don't think I should talk about that dark time," Bill said with a negative wave of his hand.

"Of course not. I'm sorry. I didn't mean to pry." But of course she did — she was dying to know everything. She hoped Bill didn't tell Blake about this.

"Oh, you aren't doing anything wrong, sweetie. It's just a really sad story," Bill said as he got up to refill their glasses. When he returned and handed her a glass of tea, he looked at her intently. "Do you care about Blake?"

Jewell was so shocked by the question, she didn't know what to do. Since this man was obviously attached to Blake, she could hardly tell him that she was only there because she was being paid to be. But at the same time, she didn't want to say a whole bunch of mushy stuff either. It would be a lie. Gosh, she felt trapped.

"You don't have to say anything, darling," Bill told her after the silence stretched on. "I can see that I put you up against a wall there."

Still, she had to say something now. "I'm sorry, Bill. I just… it's just… Well, we've only been together a few days and the situation is…well…it's just complicated."

Bill's penetrating eyes bored into her, making her squirm in her seat.

"I understand, darling. When I was younger, people didn't play all these games they play today. If a boy liked a girl, or a girl liked a boy, they told each other. If it looked like it was going good, there was no need to draw the whole dating process out. Heck, you can know on the first date if the girl looks like she'll be the one. I married my Vivian three months after we met, because I knew there'd never be another girl for me."

"What happened?"

"The good Lord took her four years ago. I still think of her every single day, and I can't wait till I get to go and be with her again."

"I'm sure she's waiting for you right at the gates."

"Not quite yet, darling. My Vivian was always too busy to

wait around for anyone. But when it's time, she'll be there to meet me all right."

"If I may ask, how did she die?"

"In her sleep, so there was no pain. I think it was just time for her to go home. I was real angry about it for a while, but I finally accepted that someone up there knows more than I do, and I realized that being angry all the time doesn't do any good."

"You are a wise man, Bill. I'm glad I've gotten to meet you." Jewell reached out her hand and took his, smoothing his wrinkly skin with her small thumb.

"I am glad I've gotten to meet you too, darling. You remind me of my sweet Vivian. She was always so calm and just loved everyone, but if you fired her up, she would have no problem taking the hide right off you," he said with a chuckle.

"I don't normally lose my temper, but…" She didn't know how to complete that sentence.

"Don't give up on Blake. He's been through some dark times in his life. His mama wasn't fit to be a mother, and it was her fault that she and the boys' daddy died. To top that off, the three boys watched it happen," Bill said with a sigh.

"Wait! They watched their parents die? Was it a car wreck?"

"No. If only it were that easy. Blake may one day open up to you about it. If he does, then you take the time to listen. I just want you to know that he has to deal with the hard times he's known however he has to deal with them. Sometimes his bark is pretty bad, but that boy has a heart of gold. He's just managed to bury it really deep."

"He's lucky to have you in his life," Jewell told him.

"Of course he is, little missy. I'm a great man." Bill smiled at her and she knew that all talk of sadness was over.

After the two of them visited a while longer, Bill fell asleep in his recliner without giving Jewell any tasks to do. So she went outside and saw the three brothers on the roof. They were working quickly, and shingles came flying over the side of the house.

A huge dumpster sat in the driveway, one that hadn't been there when Jewell had gone inside with Bill an hour earlier. She walked over to the work truck — *Knight Construction* was stenciled on the door — and, finding a pair of gloves in the back, she put them on.

Over the next couple of hours, she picked up roofing from the ground and threw it into the dumpster. By the time the sun was getting low in the sky, she was completely exhausted, but the yard was mostly cleared of debris and she felt pretty dang good about herself.

"You don't listen too well, do you?"

Jewell turned to find Blake behind her. He wiped his forehead with a rag before looking her in the eyes.

"No," she told him. "It's always been a fault of mine."

"We'll see if I can help you change your ways," he said with more than a hint of anticipation in his smile.

"You don't have time."

"I invent time. Especially for those who need punishing." He threw down the rag and tossed his shirt back on. "Let's run back to my apartment and shower. But we had better get a move on. I want to do something tonight."

He took her hand, led her to his work truck, and practically thrust her up inside.

"Where's your car?" She just couldn't picture Blake as a truck sort of a guy.

"I had my employee take it back when he delivered the truck. We needed tools."

"Oh, makes sense," she said, at a loss of what to say next.

Everyone kept throwing her new curves, it seemed, and it was taking her overwhelmed brain time to catch up.

He didn't even say goodbye to his brothers; he just started the truck and drove out into traffic. After a few minutes, Jewell's curiosity overrode her need to be quiet.

"Where are we going?"

"That's a surprise," he replied. The eager gleam that shone in his eyes made his face look so much more handsome — not that he was a slouch in that department even in his worst of moods.

Jewell wasn't sure if she'd be nearly as excited as he was about what was coming next, but she'd already argued with him far more than she should have today, so she decided to bite her tongue — if she had to — the remainder of the night.

An hour later, she would seriously regret her choice not to argue.

CHAPTER TWENTY

J EWELL'S HEARTBEAT THRASHED in her ears as she looked at the tiny plane. She rocketed immediately into fight-or-flight mode — except that *flight* was the last thing she wanted right now. She wanted to know which way to *run*.

"Do you honestly think I'm going to get into that thing?"

"Yes. Why wouldn't you?"

"Because it's a death trap on small wheels!" Her face ashen with fear, she began to pace, trying to think of some way out. This wasn't something she could do. There was no possible way. What good would she be to her brother if she died either of a terror-induced heart attack or from landing in a fiery heap on the runway of Blake's private airstrip?

"Don't be ridiculous. I've been flying for years without even minor mishaps. My mechanics certify this plane, and it's inspected before and after each flight. If the smallest thing is wrong, the problem is fixed right away."

"I'm not going." It wasn't the first time she'd refused him outright, but it was the first time she was certain she wouldn't change her mind. She didn't know if she was more panicked at the thought of flying or at the thought of what his reaction would be. But he couldn't make her go up in that thing. Her brother wouldn't want her to.

"You can do this, Jewell. There's really nothing to fear."

"Please don't make me. I can do anything else you ask — just not this."

He was silent for a full minute before his expression changed. It wasn't anger or frustration on his face; it was patience, something she hadn't seen from him before.

"Come sit inside," he told her, holding out his hand.

"No, please," she said in a tear-choked voice.

"We won't go anywhere. I just want you to sit in the plane, feel it, see that it's not so frightening."

She eyed him with suspicion. Was this a trick? He hadn't lied to her so far, hadn't told her anything and then taken it back. Could she trust him?

Though she could barely manage even to give him her hand, she found herself being propelled forward, and then she was climbing onto the small front seat. It was at least thirty seconds before she let out her breath, and that was only because he'd left the door beside her wide open. He went around the front of the plane and climbed in beside her, his thigh touching hers as he got situated.

"See? It's not so bad," he said, his voice soothing.

"It's not bad because we aren't going anywhere," she choked out.

"Why don't you ask me some questions? I'll tell you whatever you'd like to know."

How could she ask any questions when her throat was completely closed off? Since he had fallen silent, she began looking around the plane, gazing at all the dials and knobs and screens and not knowing what any of them meant.

"There are so many buttons, so many different functions for you to perform. What if something fails? Or the screens go out? Or the wheels fall off? Heck, what if a wing pops off?" She didn't give him time to answer anything before she blurted out the next question.

He waited until she stopped, and then he sent a blinding smile her way.

"I can almost guarantee you that the wings and wheels won't pop off. They're on there pretty damn tight."

"Almost? You said *almost.*" Of course she latched on to the one worrisome word.

"I wouldn't risk my life just for a cheap thrill. I know this plane better than I know my car. I guarantee you that I will take you up in the sky and then safely land you back on solid ground. I also guarantee that you will be in pure heaven while we're up there."

"You *can't* guarantee that."

"Yes, I can, Jewell. I'm confident in my ability to control this plane, just like I control my entire life — and, for that matter, your orgasms. Even if the engine stalled, I could land us safely."

Her breathing grew quicker because she now knew that she was going to go up in this plane. The door was going to close and they were going to speed down the runway and then lift off into the sky. There would be no more talking.

Blake climbed from the plane and walked over to her side. "Trust me," he said before leaning in and coming within inches of her lips — not that she really noticed.

She felt her seat belt locking and the door closing. She should say no again, should jump from the plane, should give up on the entire thing that was happening between them, but she couldn't even breathe, let alone speak.

He was soon back in the pilot seat and saying words which

she couldn't comprehend.

"...clear prop..."

"...pressure good..."

"....cleared for takeoff..."

And then they were moving. The small Cirrus emerged from Blake's personal hangar and sat at the end of his runway while the engine revved, gaining power. Jewell's eyes were wet with worry, her vision blurred. Then they started forward; the small plane quickly picked up speed.

As the plane lifted off and rapidly rose up, up, up in the sky, she held her breath, and she was sure her face was turning blue. She had no doubt that they were going to come down in a fiery blaze of glory. Where would that leave Justin?

As they climbed higher, a gust of wind shook the plane, and her hand shot out and gripped Blake's thigh. Her throat closed again and she was unable even to think any longer. A cry for help? Not possible. Who could help her anyway? They had no 911 number for the sky. Maybe he could try a mayday call over the radio, but what good would that do?

Then the most amazing thing happened. After making a large arc, Blake leveled the plane off and faced it toward the setting sun. The sky was filled with color, and his softly spoken words registered in her brain.

"Look at that. Just take a deep breath, and look."

She couldn't tear her gaze away from the view. She knew they were barreling through the evening air, but it felt like they were barely moving. The only sound she heard was his whispered words through her headset, and the only thing she could see was the brilliant reds and oranges lighting up the horizon.

"It's spectacular," she said, jumping slightly when she heard her own words echo back into her ears.

They were both too awed to say anything else as they zoomed along and watched the sun set, and then they were in the pitch-black sky, flying over fields and small cities. Blake reached down and adjusted the lights on the dashboard, and Jewell turned to see the glow outlining his handsome face.

His eyes were shining as he looked intently forward, his lips turned up in an almost secret smile, a smile that told her he was happy, he was where he belonged. He loved this — it was obvious. Her fear then evaporated because she realized she was safe. She realized that she trusted his word, trusted him to protect her.

And that filled her with an entirely new fear.

"I've always loved to fly," he said, "from the very first moment I sat left seat and took the controls of the airplane for the first time — that was when I was twenty-one and taking lessons. But my favorite time of all is at night. Everything after the sun sets feels different. It's like the rest of the world has disappeared and I'm free. Free from the chaos, the noise, the work, the anger — free from it all. I'm up here and my worries disappear for the hour or two — or five — that I decide to stay in the sky."

"I wouldn't think a guy like you, a guy who holds the world in the palm of his hand, would have a single worry you needed to forget about," she replied, her own voice quiet, not wanting to shatter this moment. Right after saying it, her conversation with Bill popped into her head, making her regret her words, especially when he snapped at her.

"I don't," he said almost harshly, but then she could hear his clear sigh through the headset. "Sorry, Jewell. I…it's just that I have to be perfect. I have to do everything right. That's what's expected, and that's who I am."

She turned and looked out the window, fighting tears. "I don't expect anything from you, Blake. I know that when our time is up, you will be gone and I will move on to whatever comes next. But thank you for helping me beat my fears, and thank you for sharing this with me."

He turned toward her, his eyes gleaming as their gazes connected. "You are a dangerous woman, Jewell. You make me think things, feel things, and do things, that I can't and don't want to do."

His words seeped in and a deep sadness overtook her. This man was holding in a past full of what had to be indescribable pain. But she was nothing to him, and she didn't need to know his secrets. They had only a few more days together. That was all. And in that time, she couldn't fall for him. It was an impossible situation.

When shutters went over his eyes, she almost felt relief. She couldn't afford to become acquainted with Blake's vulnerable side or to start to care about him. She had to remember that. If she forgot, she risked being burned so badly, she'd never be able to heal.

So when he spoke next, she shut off her heart, and let her body take over.

"Take off your clothes, Jewell."

"Of course, Blake. I was wondering when you would go back to being yourself." She unlatched her seat belt and stared him straight in the eyes while unbuttoning her blouse. What was about to happen had nothing to do with caring.

He flinched at her words, but the expression was gone so quickly, she thought she'd imagined it. He programmed something on the screen in front of him, and Jewell lost one more small piece of herself as her shirt fell from her shoulders.

CHAPTER TWENTY-ONE

BLAKE'S BREATHING STUTTERED. He was watching Jewel out of the corner of his eye as she took her sweet time stripping off her clothes. Her body was a thing of beauty. Would he ever want any other woman again?

He suspected the answer would be a flat *no*.

"Lean your seat all the way back," he said, his voice strained.

Jewell searched for the controller on the side of the seat and then slowly, surely, her seat moved back, and her body was stretched out there for his eyes to feast upon. Setting the plane on autopilot as they drifted high in the sky over empty fields, he turned and took his fill of her beauty.

He ran his hands down her smooth skin, pausing to feel the peak of her nipples jut against his palm. His groin throbbed instantly. Trailing down the slight indent of her stomach, he slid his fingers slowly along the slick folds of her core, and nearly lost control when he felt how hot, wet and ready for him she already was.

When he slipped two fingers inside her, the echo of her groan filled the small cabin. Her scent was driving him mad.

He needed her now, but the last thing he wanted was for this to go quickly. Hell, if they crashed, at least he would die one very happy man. Screw his earlier guarantees.

Reluctantly withdrawing his hand, he yanked his shirt off, tossing it somewhere onto the backseat, then unbuckled his seat belt and began undoing his jeans. He looked over and took pride in the knowledge that Jewell was watching him take off his clothing as avidly as he had watched her. There was a difference between them, though, and her innocence and curiosity acted as a complete and utter turn-on.

Sliding his seat back as far as it would go, he took a moment to catch his breath. "Take me in your mouth." His voice didn't come out nearly as strong as he wanted it to, but he was past the point of caring.

Sex with this woman was an experience he'd have difficulty finding again. Though untutored, she seemed to know instinctively what to do. He had to grip himself and squeeze to tame the pulsing when she sat up, her hair drifting over her shoulders and playing hide and seek with her breasts.

Jewell leaned over the seat between them, and her ass rose in the air as her head descended. He threw his head back when her hot mouth circled around the tip of his arousal and she sucked hard, making him lurch upward on his seat.

He gripped her ass with one hand while holding the back of her neck with the other as she slowly moved up and down his arousal. He cried out in pleasure. But as things grew too intense for him — he came close to ending this moment much too soon.

"Enough," he said after she licked his entire length, then sucked his tip again, groaning in pleasure at the task.

She let him go slowly, turning her head, her cheeks flushed as she looked up at him, her eyes shining, her nipples brushing against his thighs. She was the most beautiful creature he'd ever seen in his life.

He grasped her hips, pulled her over to him, and he sat her on his lap with her back to him.

"We can't do this — the plane will crash," she gasped, though her stomach shook beneath his hand and her head fell back, passion in her tone.

"It's on autopilot, and there's not another plane around for miles," he assured her, not that he'd let anything stop him right now. If he had to do an emergency landing in a cornfield to finish this, he'd damn well do it, but he'd never before made love while flying, and that's all he could think of doing right then.

Unable to wait even a minute more, he lifted her up, and then pushed her inch by delicious inch down onto his ready erection, completely filling her. When he didn't move for several long moments, she began to grind her hips seductively against him, her body obviously quivering with the need for release.

"Wait!" he ordered her. He needed just a moment to regain control.

She fell still as he slid his hands up her stomach and then clasped her breasts, kneading her sweet flesh before pinching the nipples and making her cry out again.

When she began once more to move up and down on him, he couldn't even think about stopping her any longer. Her slick heat coated him, so he held her tight as he felt pressure build low in his stomach and his hardness pulse inside her.

Leaning forward, he sucked the smooth skin of her neck, then ran his tongue along her shoulder, delighting in her taste, in the way her skin felt against his lips and tongue. "You make me lose my mind," he whispered in her ear, and a shudder rushed through her as he grasped her hips and set the pace for their movements, guiding her now instead of following her lead.

When their rhythm was in perfect sync, he ran a hand back up her stomach and took hold of one of her breasts, squeezing the flesh, rubbing her nipple, and the hardness of its peak made him even more aroused. His other hand found the slick bump that would make her fall into glory.

He rubbed her there, making her pant while she continued her little dance upon him, and then he lost all sense of time as wild sensations rushed through him. Their bodies glistened with a fine layer of sweat, and he kept tormenting and delighting two of her crucial pleasure points while still sucking on the honeyed skin of her neck.

"Blake!" she cried out, and he felt the tight grip of her core as her body began convulsing around him with exquisite tightness.

Blake thrust deep inside her and then groaned loudly as he let go, feeling his release wash all the way through him, making his vision blur and his head light.

"Ouch!"

Blake was startled by her exclamation. "What's wrong?" He was frustrated that he was barely able to speak.

"My knee hit the dash."

She was limp against him, utterly exhausted, her voice coming out weak, and he sagged against the seat as he tried to recover.

"You'll live," he said with a chuckle, fully relaxed.

"I don't think I'm afraid of flying anymore," she finally said.

And that's when everything went wrong.

The stall horn sounded in the cabin of the plane, alerting them that they were no longer engaged in autopilot. She must have hit the switch when her knee banged against the dash. Before he was able to respond to the alert, the plane tipped to one side and went nose down, sending them into a spin.

Jewell let out a gasp of shock, but he didn't have time to focus on it. He grabbed her waist and thrust her back to her side of the plane. Going on instinct, he slid his seat back into place so he could reach the rudders, then reached forward and took the controls. They were up high and he had plenty of time to get the plane flying again, he told himself — though he also knew everything could go bad in no time at all.

Jewell's body was thrown against his side as the plane spiraled toward the earth, making him lose his grip on the yoke for just a single second.

"Hold on!" Blake yelled when she tried scooting away. He couldn't hold out his hand to her, couldn't keep her safe *and* stop the spin. She went still against her seat, her body pressed against his side, and he moved quickly, knowing he had to get this plane back under his control.

Reducing the power back to an idle, Blake pushed against the rudder control in the opposite direction from the spin, then quickly applied full forward pressure on the controls to break the stall. Once he'd broken the stall, he held the rudder in nose-down attitude, and he didn't take his first real breath until the plane's spinning eased and then stopped. Even though this was something he had practiced several times, he had never gotten to experience it in a real-life situation and never had another person's life in his hands.

It wasn't a pleasant experience with her there. He was sure he would be getting a thrill from it if he were alone. But then again, if he were alone, it never would have happened — accidentally, at least.

The craft finally leveled off, and both of them were breathing heavily. Jewell sat frozen against her seat, gripping his arm, her nails leaving bruises and possibly breaking some skin, but with not so much as a finger twitching, while he pulled up on the yoke and brought the plane back up to altitude before he turned toward home.

Maybe mixing sex and flying wasn't such a good idea.

Nope. He couldn't think that even now, not even after nearly plummeting to the earth. It had been just too damn great.

"You can get dressed," he said, making sure to keep his voice calm.

"I…I…uh…don't know if I can move," she replied, her voice barely more than a squeak.

"We're fine, Jewell. Spins happen. Pilots are trained for them," he said, not particularly shaken up by the near disaster.

"Well, I'm not trained for it," she said, her voice stronger. Her anger came through loud and clear.

"Give me some time," he said with a chuckle, but his laughter faded away. If there was one thing that he and Jewell did not have, it was time. They had only a few days left, and then he would never see her again.

Suddenly his joy of flying, his joy of making love in the sky, his joy of it all disappeared. Jewell Weston had gotten underneath his skin, and he had a feeling it would be a long time before he was able to purge her from his system.

"Put your clothes on, Jewell. Our flight is over."

Blake's fear of falling for her made him much crueler than he needed to be, but he had to protect himself. If she knew how vulnerable she made him, she would hold power over him, and that was unacceptable.

CHAPTER TWENTY-TWO

EVEN THOUGH THE night before had ended on a rather sour note, Jewell still found herself locked in Blake's arms, his hands rubbing along her naked back, as she woke up early the next morning...it was Wednesday. She had only four more nights left with this man, and though he didn't deserve her affections, a piece of her would always belong to him.

That frightened her.

"So tell me, Jewell, why are you doing this? You're clearly not stupid, and though it's not easy to find jobs in this economy, you don't seem the sort of woman to stoop so low, to sell your body."

"We've discussed this before, you know."

"And we'll discuss it again. Tell me the real reason you're doing this."

"You wouldn't believe me, Blake. And I don't want this to get back to Ms. Beaumont. Let's just say that I have my reasons and leave it at that."

"If you have nothing to hide, then tell me. I might well believe you."

She took a breath, fighting with whether to say anything. She wanted to speak about Justin, to have someone understand, and for some reason, she wanted Blake to know she wasn't some scarlet woman. But at the same time she feared he would quickly turn on her.

"Maybe I just like to screw different men," she said as cavalierly and as crudely as she could. His arms tensed around her and she knew her answer hadn't pleased him.

"I don't buy that, Jewell. You were a virgin. Women don't just wake up one day and decide to turn tricks. There has to be something behind it. We're you hoping to hook yourself a billionaire?" He asked the question as if the answer had to be a simple yes.

That sure as heck ignited her wrath. Why did he always have to go for the jugular, to say the meanest thing he could think of?

"Does it give you pleasure to be so rude? Maybe we're a lot alike. Maybe I did want to hook a billionaire. Maybe I will indeed do just that," she said, not believing she'd just been about ready to tell him about Justin. That could be a fatal mistake if his attitude was any indication.

Blake fastened on her question. "Yes, it usually does please me to be an ass. That way people know where they stand. They don't have any expectations of me."

The slight vulnerability in his tone made her want to open up a bit more to him. She thought back to her conversation with Bill and the pain Blake and his brothers had suffered. She really wanted to know that story, but she had a feeling today wasn't going to be the day she learned what happened back then. She probably never would find out how his parents died. So she decided to tell him nothing.

"Well, since we're only together for four more nights, Blake, you don't have to worry about my intentions. We will go our separate ways and never have to bother each other again." She really wasn't sure how she was feeling about that.

He wasn't the devil. She didn't know exactly who or what he was, but she was certain that she could have been set up with someone much worse than he was. At least his company didn't repulse her and at least the sex was beyond anything she could have ever imagined sex feeling like.

But sex wasn't enough. Sure, it was wonderful in the moment, but when it was over, emptiness swamped her, even while lying in his arms, because she knew it wasn't where she was supposed to be, knew that he would have another woman lying there with him before the bedsheets even grew cold.

"Do you think I like repeating myself, Jewell? But I will. *Tell me why you are doing this.*"

"You really don't give up, do you?"

"No. You should know this by now."

"Fine… I have a brother. A younger brother."

He paused as if taken aback by her words. Whatever he'd expected to hear, it most certainly wasn't that. She practically held her breath as she waited for him to comment.

"He must be very proud of his big sister," he finally said, his words dripping with sarcasm.

"If he ever found out, I'd… Oh, I just can't imagine what I'd do. But I have no other choice. I have to do what I'm doing now. There isn't another option, any other way. I have looked and looked for work…" She trailed off when she saw his body grow increasingly tense. He wasn't her friend. He didn't want to hear her story. That was more than obvious.

He surprised her, though, when he spoke again. "No other way to what?"

Maybe he did care, if only the slightest bit. After all, he wasn't a man who lacked any proper emotion. And it was clear how much he cared about his own two brothers, so why wouldn't he understand her love for Justin?

"To get him back. He's in foster care, and I need to get money fast so the judge will let me keep him. I couldn't get a job anywhere else, so—"

Blake cut her off. "You were right, dammit. That's the worst B.S. I've ever heard. I'm sure that every hooker on this wretched planet works up a little sob story like that."

"But it's not a—"

"Yes, Jewell, it is a sob story. You know I'm a wealthy man. You want a piece of that wealth. Did you really think I would be affected by your lie and hand you a bunch of cash so you can go out and get your next fix, or whatever it is that is driving you to work as a common…okay, an expensive prostitute? I thought maybe you would try honesty, but obviously you're not capable of that."

"Why in the world did you even ask if you weren't going to believe me?" she said, fighting the urge to cry. Why his lecture even mattered she would never know.

"I guess I'm a fool, because I was almost taken in a little by the innocence I've seen in your eyes. You are very good at looking like the girl next door — like a lost little puppy who needs to be taken care of. But I guarantee you that I can't be fooled," he said, sounding almost proud of himself.

"Well, I'm so glad you have me all figured out, Mr. Knight," she told him, her body stiff next to him. She knew that was something he wouldn't tolerate.

And he didn't. He quickly flipped her onto her back and covered her body, staring down into her face, refusing to release her eyes as he made it abundantly clear which one of the two of them was in charge.

"Stop it now, Jewell. If you ever mention this lie again, I'll send you straight back to McKenzie — Ms. Beaumont to you — and tell her you're a liar who can't be trusted. Liars never get anywhere in life. Remember that. I'll even tell her what you're lying about. You're not too smart, after all," he said with a sneer.

"Don't worry. I won't even think of telling you anything again." How she hated that her traitorous body was responding to his even when he was belittling her.

"I'm not worried, Jewell," he assured her. "There's nothing you could do or say that would ever make me feel that emotion."

Then before she was able to reply, he pushed forward, sinking inside her and making her gasp in outrage as she glared at him even as her body responded.

"I own you, Jewell," he said, his eyes shining with victory.

"For four more days," she said, unable to hold back the words that furthered his anger.

He leaned forward and shut her mouth the best way he knew how. Although she couldn't help but kiss him back, Jewell hated him and herself just a little bit more over the next hour.

When they were finished, she knew she'd been used, but that was what she was there for. He stood up and dressed, making her feel even cheaper.

"By the way, you have a dress fitting in an hour or so. We'll be attending a function on Friday night and you need proper attire."

He didn't wait for her response, but instead left the room. She got up, showered and made her way down the stairs, surprised to find him sitting there. Looking at the clock, she knew the person coming over to help her would be there soon.

"Why aren't you at work?" It was a natural question, as he was normally gone by now.

"I decided to take most of the week off. I want to get my money's worth," he said, not glancing up from the tablet he was most likely reading the paper on. "You should be happy. You've complained about being watched on camera, so you're free from that for now. Just watching was taking up too much of my time, anyway."

She didn't bother with a response to that, not understanding his sudden need to hurt her. He'd asked her to tell him the truth, and she had, and now she was being punished for that. It didn't seem fair to her at all.

When the doorbell rang after half an hour of uncomfortable silence, she was almost relieved, but when a petite woman walked in, with an assistant behind her dragging a rack that had several dresses on it, Jewell tensed up all over again.

A dress fitting — really? Just one more thing in a long line of things she had never thought she would have any part of before. It was okay, though. It wouldn't be so bad to go to some stuffy event. It wasn't as if she would ever socialize again with any of the people who attended.

"You must be Jewell," the woman said, then proceeded to look her up and down with what seemed to be a suppressed sneer, and circled around her. Jewell wanted desperately to fidget.

When Blake sat down on the couch and leaned back, she felt like screaming. He was going to just sit there the entire time and make her even more uncomfortable. Why? This couldn't be his idea of a good time.

"I need you to strip down to your panties," the woman said as she pulled out a tape measure.

"Excuse me?" Jewell looked over to the young man who was standing silently by the clothing rack.

"I need you to strip down to your panties," she repeated as if she were dealing with a small, disobedient child.

Jewell was about to throw a fit, so maybe she was a child,

indeed.

"Um, can we go into the bathroom, or something?" Jewell asked as she again looked at the young man — a kid, really — and then at Blake, who wasn't even looking at the tablet anymore, his attention now fully focused on her.

"No. I need the light in this room. You're wasting my time, Jewell," the woman said, and she took a step closer.

Jewell had no doubt that if she didn't strip, the woman would do it for her. And *that* wasn't going to happen.

She began taking off her clothes, trying to remind herself that this kid had to have seen it all before. It didn't help ease her humiliation one bit, however. When she was down to her panties, which didn't cover much, Jewell closed her eyes and stood there awkwardly while the woman told her to hold out her arms, and move this way and that.

By the time the measurements were all finished, she had been touched and poked, and the woman had even had the gall to comment on some of her troubled areas. Jewell didn't know how she managed to hold back the scream lodging in her throat.

She refused to make eye contact with Blake, but she was sure the jerk was thoroughly enjoying himself at her expense. Her week with him couldn't end soon enough.

Next came a show of dresses. Of course there wasn't time to make one from scratch. She'd have to choose one, and then the woman would tailor it to her body. Blake rejected dress after dress, and by the eighth one she was sick of slipping them on and off.

"No. That one isn't right. Didn't I give you specific directions on what I wanted?" Blake snapped.

The woman's nose turned up an inch higher at that comment, and Jewell was surprised. She hadn't though sticking that snoot up higher were humanly possible.

"I assure you that I have never not pleased a client, Mr. Knight," she said, her tone respectful even if her expression wasn't.

She pulled out another dress and he sat forward. "That one," he said before Jewell even had a chance to try it on.

"Let's see how it looks," the woman said in a warning tone as the young man slid it over Jewell's head.

The material was similar to a few she'd already tried on, but the fit was better, even without any tailoring. It dipped low in front and back and ended high on her thighs, but it almost felt like she was wearing nothing at all, it was so light.

"Yes, that's the one."

The boy helped Jewell out of the dress, and she stood there with her arms crossed, trying to protect her naked body from their view, even though they'd all been staring at her shamelessly for the past hour.

"I'll have the dress ready by Friday morning," the woman said before making a quick exit.

Jewell finally breathed. She moved over to her discarded clothes and gathered them to go upstairs.

"Meet me in my room."

She didn't even bother looking at him as she moved to the staircase. This day just wasn't ever going to end. The really depressing part of it all was that although she knew she was his sex toy, and she knew he had no respect for her, she also knew she would enjoy their lovemaking. She assured herself that each time it was finished, she would also hate him that much more.

CHAPTER TWENTY-THREE

"OOOH, THAT'S GOING to leave a mark!"
Jewell spewed out water as she pulled herself back up on the wakeboard. She then sent a glare straight to Tyler, who was so busy laughing as he looked back at her that she hoped he choked on his own tongue.

"Don't worry about me. I'm just fine," she snapped, determined to master this ridiculous sport.

"I wasn't worried," Tyler assured her as he waited until she was holding the rope in her hands and her feet were firmly planted back on the wakeboard. He held up his hand and Blake put the boat back into full throttle as she struggled to get up on her feet.

They were at the lake, and had been there for the past three hours. She hadn't spoken a single word to Blake since they'd left his apartment, and she'd be more than pleased to continue not speaking to him for the next four nights, not after what an absolute ass he'd been to her that morning.

He was the one who had asked her why she was doing this job, and then he'd treated her horribly when she'd spoken the truth. Let him think she was a liar. The alternative was having him know about Justin and telling the whole story to Ms. Beaumont. That wasn't an option. She couldn't believe she'd had such a weak moment as to open up to him.

What had he done in the past few days to prove to her that she could trust him? Absolutely nothing. She'd been a fool, but it wouldn't happen again. At least she didn't have to be alone with him right now — and maybe he'd even planned this outing because he, too, didn't want to be alone with her. Anyway, she actually enjoyed Tyler's company. Granted, she wasn't as happy being around Byron. He was just as stern and bitter as Blake, so they weren't the best people to hang out with on a hot, sunny day on the lake.

Before she could move on to another thought, she felt herself go under again. Water immediately flooded into her open mouth and panicked her for a moment.

When she came back up, coughing out water and taking in much-needed oxygen, she decided she was finished with this so-called sport. Weren't sports supposed to be fun? Taking her feet out of the boots on the wakeboard, she waited for the fancy black boat to circle back around to her, and then swam toward it.

"Are you giving up already, gorgeous?" Tyler asked as he held out a hand to help her up.

"I don't think I'll be able to walk in the morning. I'm done," she almost gasped, irritated that she was so out of breath, she collapsed onto one of the benches in the back of the boat.

"You aren't giving yourself enough credit. You got up and lasted a while," Tyler told her, beaming a proud smile her way and actually bringing a glow to her cheeks.

Blake approached the two of them. "Would you quit flirting with my girl?" he said gruffly.

"Oh, come on, Blake. I like Jewell. She's a real trouper," Tyler told him. Winking at his brother, he sat down at Jewell's feet, lifted them into his lap, and began to knead the tender flesh on the soles and around the arches. She moaned appreciatively.

"Get your hands off her," Blake growled, and he pushed his brother away.

Jewell wanted to protest the interruption of her foot rub, but with the thunderclouds obvious in Blake's eyes, she decided she was much better off remaining silent.

"You're such a stick in the mud," Tyler said with a gigantic grin. "All right, Byron, looks like Blake's out for driving. You're at the helm now. Give her hell." He grabbed his board and jumped into the water.

Blake still didn't say anything directly to Jewell as they raced around the lake, but he also didn't move away, making Jewell shift involuntarily while he sat there beside her, his hand on her leg, obviously staking his claim in front of his brothers.

She didn't see why he would even bother. He'd made it clear that he had no particular fondness for her, and certainly no respect.

"Are you going to continue to give me the silent treatment the rest of the day?" he finally asked, startling her.

"I'm just minding my own business, Blake." She knew that if she didn't reply, he could and would continue to push her.

"I don't like it, Jewell, so stop."

"Well then, what should we talk about? We are civilized people, after all," she remarked with more than just a hint of sarcasm dripping from her tongue.

He leaned in close, his eyes narrowed into slits. "I won't tolerate you speaking to me this way, especially in front of my brothers."

"I'm surprised you don't just tell them that I'm your personal prostitute, and that our time is almost over, that they can have a turn next if they wait until Monday." Where was this cattiness coming from? Jewell hadn't a clue, but she suspected she'd come to regret it. And when he leaned toward her, rage burning in his eyes, she knew she would. And soon.

"They already know," he said, making her humiliation complete before he continued speaking. "Is that what you want, Jewell? Do you want to be bedded by all three of us? Right now? Want me to find a nice quiet little alcove? Or wait, you like the public stuff, don't you? Why don't I just find a place where all the boats are tied together and you can make your rounds? Don't worry, doll — I know you expect to be paid extra for taking on multiple partners. Not a problem."

The sneer on his face made her want to slap him. Oh how she would love to wipe away his arrogance, if only for a single second.

"I'm not the whore you make me into," she found herself saying, her throat tight.

"Then quit making comments that make you seem like one," he fired back. "You're your own *sales*woman, you know."

"Why don't we just go back to not speaking? You are so much more pleasant that way."

Before she could say anything else, he pulled her up and straddled her over his lap. "Don't even think for one minute that because I allow you to speak your mind, I give a damn about your opinion," he said before crushing his mouth punishingly against hers.

When the boat stopped, Tyler climbed back on board and gave a catcall. Blake immediately pulled away, and she could still see the rage he'd been directing at her flashing in his silver depths.

She had to fight the urge to cry, but there was no way she

was doing that again. She'd shed enough tears in the last six months to last her a lifetime, and Blake Knight was certainly not worth wasting any of her precious emotions on.

He released her and stood. "I'm done. Let's go back in," he said to Byron, who was now captain of the boat.

Everyone fell silent. The boat turned, and Jewell was relieved when they came closer to the docks. The sooner this horrible day ended, the better off she would be. Then she'd be tied to Blake for only three more nights.

Tyler gave her a questioning look, but even he said nothing. And now they were at the docks, and Blake was leading her up the ramp and straight to his car.

Their night seemed destined to be less than pleasant. When he sent her to her room and didn't even try to bring her to his bed or join her in hers, she was relieved, or she thought she was. As she gazed at the clock next to her bed and sleep didn't easily find her, she felt nothing but despair. She told herself it was because she was counting the endless hours until her release from this nightmare, and freedom from Blake Knight was still so far away.

CHAPTER TWENTY-FOUR

TICKTOCK, TICKTOCK, THE time was counting down.

Barely able to climb from her bed, her muscles were so sore, Jewell somehow managed to stumble into her bathroom. Though he'd told her yesterday that he was taking the rest of the week off, she hoped that after their tiff Blake would be at work the entire day and that she could cross one more day with him off her calendar.

After showering, she made her way painfully down the stairs and went straight to the coffeepot. The apartment was quiet and she was relieved to realize she was alone. He was his own boss, so he could take any day off he wanted — like yesterday — and she simply couldn't predict what the man might decide to do next. It threw her too far off balance for her comfort. But today he must have gone to his headquarters. She would be free at least until the evening.

As she finished her first cup of coffee, she heard the familiar ding of her phone — the darn thing was sitting on the kitchen counter — and she grimaced.

She needed just five more minutes, maybe one hour, to wake up and get her armor in place before speaking to Blake. Please, she begged, please... But when it dinged again almost immediately, she knew that to avoid whatever he had to say would be foolish. And it would be texting, nothing more.

She was still going to assert some shred of independence. She went over to the coffeepot first, filled her cup, and added a nice splash of cream to it before taking a sip. The third message came in and she finally forced herself to go over to her phone.

Good morning, Jewell, I hope you slept well.

That message confused her. He'd been such a jackass the day before; why would he send something civilized like that? It made no sense to her. Maybe the man was bipolar. Or maybe he even suffered from multiple personality disorder. That wouldn't surprise her in the least.

Be ready in one hour. I'll be picking you up.

Her stomach tightened. She didn't want to spend the day with him. It was going to be awkward and unpleasant, and she would just end up feeling bad about herself again. It could be a lot worse, though. She had to remind herself of the stories she'd heard from the other escorts. At least she wasn't being tied up to things and flogged, or being forced to have sicko sex in front of an audience.

Get over your tantrum, Jewell, and·get ready... Now!

Tantrum? What freaking universe did he inhabit? Or did he own a special cyber helmet that made every jerky thing he did look and smell like roses?

Fine! Jewell punched in each of those letters in her one-word response with no little savagery, and dropped the phone on the counter, delighting when it bounced. She took her coffee cup with her back up the stairs and walked into her closet to find clothes. She had no idea what he was planning and didn't know how to dress, so she chose a skirt that came halfway down her thighs, and a tank top that revealed her back but at least didn't show most of her breasts. She wouldn't make it into a "sideboob" photo gallery.

Forty-five minutes later, she heard the sound of a key turning in the lock on the front door, and she rolled her eyes. It wouldn't take long for her to discover what was coming up next in this weeklong adventure with Blake.

"Hello, Jewell. You look lovely today, but you always do."

She stood there dumbfounded. He was behaving so differently than he normally did when he was around her. Was this a trick? She had no clue what to think right now.

He smiled as if knowing he was confusing her, and approached her with the confidence she'd come to expect from him. "When a person says hello and offers a compliment, the correct response is usually to offer a greeting in return."

Then he pulled her into his arms and, before she was able to say a word, he kissed her. It wasn't a greedy assault on her mouth, but a soft, drugging kiss that made her legs tremble in weakness. When he moved back and looked into her eyes, she found she was still too stunned to speak. It had now been an uncomfortable, silent couple of minutes, and she really felt stupid.

"We're going out today for a walk," he said, and released her to wobble on her own as he grabbed her light jacket, which was hanging on the back of the chair. She still hadn't said a word as he helped her slip it on.

Finally, she found her voice. "What is going on?"

"Nothing. I told you I was taking the week off, but I needed to go in for a few hours to take care of things. I've finished and now I want to stretch my legs," he said, and he led her out the front door.

"It's not much of a week off if you still go in to the offices," she pointed out.

"I'm the owner. There are certain things that only my brothers or I can do."

She was surprised he was even bothering to explain any of this to her. She was surprised by his attitude change altogether. He was almost treating her like a human being instead of his plaything. She would do best to remember this wasn't typical.

They made their way outside, where his driver, Max, was waiting. Jewell said nothing as he helped her into the backseat and then joined her. They drove for several hours, chatting about nothing of importance, and she finally found herself relaxing in his presence. She didn't even care where they were going. He'd said a walk, but so far the only walking they'd done had been from the elevator to the car.

When the driver stopped, then quickly came around and opened her door, she was surprised to find herself at a winery and vineyard.

"We're going to a fundraiser tomorrow night, as you know. I thought I would give you a sampling of good wines while we stretched our legs."

Blake obviously thought she was a newbie to any wine that needed a corkscrew to open, but she wasn't going to get all huffy about it. He was pretty much right.

Soon the two of them moved through the vineyard. They stopped at several stations to taste the local wines associated with each variety of grape being grown, some of which left a sour taste in her mouth, and some of which she wanted much more of.

After an hour, he led her to a private balcony off the main lodge restaurant, where a table was already set with wineglasses; food arrived not long thereafter.

"I've spent some time mulling over what you said yesterday, Jewell, and I think I jumped too quickly to an unfavorable conclusion."

Her heart started thundering. Did he believe her? She was too fearful to even voice the question.

His next words made her glad she hadn't.

"Though I don't believe your story, I do believe that there's a story you aren't sharing with me. I would like to know what it is," he said levelly.

She'd had so many tastes of wine — she really should have spit them out like the experts! — that she had to fight past the fog her brain was in. Sure, the glasses had been small and they were far from full, but she must have had the equivalent of four to six full glasses. She really needed to eat some of the food before her if she wanted to come close to keeping up with him.

"I thought you told me you didn't care about my story, Blake."

"I shouldn't care in the least, Jewell, but oddly enough, I find myself wanting to know more about you."

"Why? Our time is nearly up — as if I need to remind you of that again. There's nothing else you need to know about me." She picked up a piece of bread and began eating it, hoping it would soak up some of the alcohol she'd already downed. She didn't dare touch the wineglass in front of her.

"Just because our time is almost up doesn't mean we can't have a conversation. Sunday hasn't arrived yet."

"Well, I just want to get through the next few days," she told him. Those words were truer than any other she'd spoken to him.

His smile evaporated and he looked at her intently. "I am trying to be pleasant. I don't appreciate it that you're not putting in the effort to do the same."

"You can't just flip a switch all of a sudden and expect me to pour out my heart to you. It was only a few days ago that you told me to do my job and not to even think of feeling anything about you."

"Maybe I've changed my mind about that," he said.

She looked at him in utter horror. That had to be sarcasm; it couldn't be anything else.

His eyes turned a bit colder after seeing her response, but otherwise showed no emotion. "So you would rather I treat you as nothing but an object, something I've bought — no, rented?"

"Yes, I do. That would be best for both of us."

"Fine, Jewell. You want that. You have it," he said, and a dangerous gleam appeared in his eyes.

Their lunch was forgotten. Blake stood and held out a hand, not as a courtesy but as a command. Her stomach dipped. But she took his hand, and when she did, she swayed on her feet. Where was he going to lead her?

When they ended up in a small basement room in the large house overlooking the winery, she felt panic coming on. And with reason.

"Strip for me, Jewell. That's what you're so good at."

The color drained from her face. She was a prostitute. It was for the best that he was reminding her of that fact. Trying to erase all thoughts, all emotions, to become nothing but a robot, a sex toy, she began taking off her clothes. That only dim lanterns lit the room was of small consolation.

By the time they left, Blake had stripped another piece of her soul away.

CHAPTER TWENTY-FIVE

TWO NIGHTS!

That's how much time she had remaining with this man. Only two more nights. Jewell knew that she shouldn't be elated, filled with a sense of euphoria — after all, it wasn't as if freedom awaited her. She'd have to go back to Relinquish Control, and who knew what sort of man Blake's successor would be? She'd really meant to give this all up, but getting custody of Justin would be so much easier if she had more money. But Blake had made her realize, she really was just a whore.

There was no reason for her to be standing in the shower feeling almost as if doom were hanging over her head. Something more had to be going on with her.

No, she wasn't falling in love with Blake. That would be impossible. He'd barely shown her *any* kindness. Yes, he'd held her close after the plane nearly crashed — though he insisted he'd had it under control — and at other times, she'd seen small moments of softness in him, but not nearly enough.

No. If anything, any time he showed the barest amount of

humanity, he would quickly mask it by letting the dominant, controlling part of his personality take over. She still felt dirty after their "tryst" at the winery. He'd taken his pleasure within her against a wine barrel, and he'd done it in total silence. So she *was* relieved to be leaving him. She just wasn't relieved to be going back to the cold building where the next man would choose her as if she were nothing more than a piece of cattle up for sale. That had to be the source of the doom.

After taking her time in the shower, she took even more time getting ready for the evening. This was no stay-at-home evening of TV or kinky sex. Tonight she had to go to a fundraising dinner with Blake, and the whole idea had put her stomach in a constant state of upheaval.

Jewell was about to enter a world she'd only read about. Her mother had provided a good and safe home, but they'd lived on the lower end of the middle-class spectrum. The only fundraisers they'd attended were small-potato affairs at the public school. This fundraiser would pull in millions of dollars.

Would she pass inspection when Blake came to pick her up? The mirror gave her no answers. The dress that had been tailored specifically for her was exquisite, fitting her like a glove, and in every respect far more beautiful than anything she'd ever imagined wearing. She liked it, and she would have to remember to thank him. She hoped no one would look at her and know exactly what she was, and exactly how out of place she was.

The waiting was making things worse.

His week off, thankfully, wasn't a true week off. Yes, he was taking her out some in the day, but his phone constantly rang, and he was leaving often after that, even if there was an irritated scowl on his forehead as he walked out the door. And she'd also seen no more of his texting, no more sign that he had those freaking cameras on. He'd clearly grown tired of watching her, and she really couldn't complain.

She had to admit that Blake had an incredible work ethic. It wasn't just for clients with megabucks, or from behind a desk. She'd watched him sweat away up on Bill's roof, his button-down shirt thrown off, his expensive slacks ruined, and he'd looked like he was meant to hold a hammer.

She knew that all the Knight brothers had started out on job sites before they created their own company, a business so successful that none of them should ever feel the need to do manual labor again. It showed their character that they could roll up their sleeves and help a friend, and she didn't want to be impressed, but she was. How many other billionaires were willing to climb up on a roof for a man they loved and respected? But the way Blake treated her also showed his character, and it *wasn't* something that anyone should brag about.

Yes, it was for the best that her time with Blake was nearly over. She'd had this suspicion before, and it kept growing stronger — if she were with him much longer, she'd be helpless to resist needing his attention. Those glimpses she had of vulnerability within him were trying to break through to her heart, and the sex — oh my, the sex. It was incredible.

It was funny how things had turned out. Well…maybe not exactly funny. Blake wasn't a man a woman stayed with. She felt that maybe she had a touch of Stockholm syndrome. Since she was tied to Blake, she felt she needed to be with him. Yet how could she feel that way when he could be so absolutely horrible to her? Her mother hadn't raised any masochists.

Jewell thought back to when she was fifteen and had fallen in love for the first time. What a disaster — she'd seen the boy kissing her mortal enemy behind the bleachers, and she'd come

home in tears. Her mother had consoled her, and told her that
it sometimes took a little while to find "the one," but that she'd
someday find him. The man she would marry had to be her
best friend, had to be her lover, and had to be the person she
trusted above all others. *Never settle*, her mom said. *Ask for the
moon and don't take less.*

Jewell had never found a man who fit that description.

Instead, she'd found Blake Knight, who most certainly was
none of those things. And especially not the man she would
marry — if she ever did. Yes, he was a virtuoso lover — perhaps
she should use the adjective *masterful* — but he'd never offer
her the moon or the stars. That just wasn't who he was. Besides,
she had her brother to think about; to think of her own needs
was selfish.

She finally went down the stairs. Was she supposed to wait
for him in the living room or meet him in the lobby? She didn't
know why they hadn't planned this a little better.

Going over to get her phone — once again, she'd forgotten
to keep it with her — she saw several messages and grimaced.
So she'd been wrong, at least, about the texting. He might be
tired of watching her, but not of controlling her.

> My driver will pick you up.
>
> Where are you?
>
> Max is waiting in the lobby.
>
> Jewell!

She smiled at that last message, practically hearing the
growl in his voice. It had come in ten minutes earlier. She was
surprised he hadn't added a dozen more to it. His driver was
early, dang it, so it wasn't her fault if he was kept waiting.

On my way down now. Was getting ready.

After hitting Send, she tucked the phone into her purse and did a final check in the grand mirror in the entry before she walked out the door. When she reached the lobby, she saw Max waiting and she instantly tensed. She'd almost forgotten that he knew exactly who and what she was, and it wasn't a perfect way for her to start out her big evening.

He hadn't spoken to her the other day when going to the winery. She hadn't been alone with him since that ride last Monday as a matter of fact. This would be too similar to that horrible ride with just the two of them, and she didn't need that reminder right now while she was on her way to a social event with people with more money than any one person needed.

She was already uncomfortable about going to the wretched event, and now she had to ride there with a man who most certainly looked down upon her. But since there was nothing she could do about it, she held her head high as she approached him.

"Good evening, Ms. Weston," Max said.

His slight smile shocked her.

"Good evening, Max. I'm sorry to keep you out so late."

They left the building and he opened the car door for her. She was glad the car was parked at the curb — she didn't think she could have borne going all the way down the elevator with him and then through the parking garage.

"I work all hours. It's no trouble at all," he replied.

She didn't say anything else as she climbed in and got comfortable. When Max pulled into traffic, Jewell forced herself to clear her mind of all fears. Yes, she was rubbing her skin raw as she twisted her fingers together, but that was stupid. She had no choice but to go to the fundraiser, so what good did worrying really do her? None. In fact, it was a *party*, and she might as well try to enjoy it. That was possible, wasn't it? Okay, probably not.

They arrived much sooner than she was prepared for, and she shuddered when Max helped her out of the car. And then it got worse. She looked around, but there was no sign at all of Blake, which meant she was faced with walking in alone. Would they let her in? She had nothing to show the men at the doors, nothing to prove that she was supposed to be there. What would she do if they sent her away? Her "date" — that made her smile, almost — could have had the decency to meet her at the car, at the very least.

Sighing, she forced herself forward. When did Blake ever act the gentleman? Pretty much never. She approached two men in tuxes who were guarding the entrance of this fancy hotel, and they didn't even try to smile.

"Invitation?" one asked.

"I…uh…I don't have one. I'm here with someone," she said and the answering look in his eyes clearly said he didn't believe her.

Before she could speak again, Max stepped up next to her. "She is here with Blake Knight."

The man's attitude changed instantly, and he held the door open for her. "I apologize, Ms. Weston. He's waiting for you inside."

Wow! Jewell couldn't imagine what it would be like to possess that much power with nothing but a name. She had refrained from sneaking into Blake's computer to run a Web search on his name, but maybe she would try to find out all she could after she was free of him.

Then again, maybe she wouldn't. Once their time was over,

it would be best for her to forget all about the man, to forget all about their time together.

After stepping through the front doors of the hotel and being escorted to the site of the fundraiser, Jewell was taken aback by the luxury before her. Sparkling light fixtures hung throughout the room, and the round tables were set expertly with the finest china, crystal, and what she was sure was real silver. These people clearly didn't worry about thieves — they probably didn't have to.

Waiters moved silently through the room, making sure that everyone had a fresh drink, which couldn't be an easy task — the crowd was much larger than she had expected. How was she ever going to find Blake in this throng of people?

When a woman's tinkling laughter drifted toward her, she looked toward the sound, and then felt her stomach take an instant dip. Finding Blake hadn't been so difficult after all. She just hadn't expected to find him with a woman clinging to his side. It didn't matter to her, of course. But why in the world would he ask her to get all dressed up for this glittering event just to leave her standing there alone, looking like a fool?

As if he could sense her presence, he turned his head in her direction, and their eyes collided from across the room. She must have still been frowning, because the smile on his face vanished and his eyebrows rose quizzically, and then he held out his hand and gestured for her to join him. But that woman stayed right there with him.

It wasn't awkward enough for her, no doubt, so he had to throw another woman right down her throat. But who cared, right? She was just his weeklong fling. After the week was over, she would go on to the next man, and then the next, until she had enough saved to ensure her brother could come and live with her.

That thought stopped her in her tracks. Relinquish Control wasn't a cheap place to find an escort. What if the next man attended the same parties that Blake did? How awkward would that be?

As if the thought had magically summoned unwanted people, a man bumped into her, and when he quickly turned to apologize, he stopped and stared, his words trapped in his throat.

"Um...excuse me," Jewell finally said, and she tried to brush past him.

He took hold of her arm to keep her there. "Your name is Jewell, right?"

She gulped. This was *so* not good. She'd seen this man at the agency only a day before Blake had arrived. He'd come and spoken to her, but when Ms. Beaumont had told him that she wasn't quite ready yet, he'd winked and promised to be back as soon as she was available for purchase.

Was one of the other girls there with him now?

"Yes. I really need to get going," she said, trying to pull her arm away.

"What's the rush, honey? Why don't you have a drink with me?" There was something about this man that she'd instantly disliked, and seeing him wearing a tux and holding a glass of vintage wine didn't improve that first impression.

"I'm here with someone," she said as she tried again to get free.

"I thought you weren't ready to escort anyone," he said, his smile evaporating and the tone of his words displaying a piece of his temper.

"I'm sorry for any misunderstanding, but if you could release me, I should find my date."

He leaned forward to whisper in her ear, making her

shudder in fear and loathing. "I don't see why a whore would want to rush off. It doesn't matter who you're here with tonight, because I guarantee you I'll be purchasing you and your *services* next."

She didn't know how to respond to such a man, and she felt her throat close. He was right. She didn't own herself, not as long as she worked for Relinquish. She was owned by whichever man paid the right price. And she would end up attending parties where multiple men knew exactly who she was. This nightmare would never end as long as she lived in Seattle.

When she got Justin out of foster care, the two of them would move far, far away, because if her brother ever found out what she was doing, he would be so disappointed in her. She would never be able to handle him looking at her the way this man was doing right then.

"Why don't we just skip all the paperwork and you come home with me now? You'll make far more money that way," he said with a smile that told her he thought he now had her in the bag.

"The lady is with me."

Jewell almost felt relief when Blake broke in and put his arm possessively around her, easily taking her away from the other man's grasp. The rage shimmering off him didn't seem to be directed at her for once.

"I'm sorry, Blake; I didn't realize she was here with you…on a…date," the man said with a wink.

"Be really careful what you say next, Steve." Blake's words were quiet, but that didn't lessen the threat.

"I wasn't saying anything," Steve hastily replied, but the leer he sent Jewell's way made her skin crawl.

"Good." With that, Blake pulled her away, and she didn't feel her heart start slowing until they were halfway across the room.

Then the beat picked right back up when the woman she'd seen him with a few minutes earlier interrupted their escape.

"Blake, aren't you going to introduce us?"

Blake stopped, and to Jewell's utter amazement, his expression softened, causing instant jealousy to rush through her veins. Who was this snake-charming woman, a woman who could enchant even Blake Knight? Not that it mattered... He wasn't hers, and she didn't want him to be.

"Jewell, this is Monica," Blake said. "Monica, Jewell, my date this evening."

Monica stuck out her hand. "It's a pleasure to meet you, Jewell."

Jewell had no choice but to shake the woman's hand — if she didn't, she'd look completely rude. So she gave the obligatory handshake, then moved back as quickly as possible.

Blake led the two women to a corner table and held out both of their chairs before seating himself between them. Though Jewell made her face a mask of unconcern, the longer she sat there with Blake and Monica, the more irate she became.

How dare he drag her down to this worthless event only to ignore her? How dare he flaunt another woman in her face? Okay, it wasn't as if she owned him. She knew she didn't. They weren't in a relationship at all. But still, it was just plain rude.

After they finished dinner, when Blake asked Jewell for a dance, she was less than enthusiastic, but she had to admit feeling just the slightest bit of satisfaction that he was asking her and not Monica first. Though she was sure he would trade them off quickly.

She was stiff in his arms when he tried to pull her close, and he looked down at her with puzzlement in his face. "Are you not having a nice night? I know these events can be slightly dry, but the music is good, and the food was better than most. This isn't the rubber-chicken circuit."

"I'm fine," she said, her words clipped.

He stopped in the middle of the dance floor, not caring if anyone noticed them. "Jewell, there's obviously something wrong. Is it that man?" he asked as his eyes scanned the room.

"No. He's nobody," she said, surprised she'd forgotten about Steve in her uncomfortable time at the table with Blake and Monica.

"Tell me *now*, Jewell!" He wasn't being as kind now; the domineering Blake had taken over again.

"Fine! I think it's very rude of you to bring me down here when you already had a date. How many does one guy need? Especially since you and Monica seem to get along so well," she snapped. Then her eyes flew wide open and she bit down on her lips, wishing she could sew them shut.

His expression went from shock to confusion and then, to her utter outrage, to amusement. His lips turned up and before she could say another word, he let out a soft chuckle, and that degenerated into full-blown laughter.

"I'm not going to stand here and take this," she told him. There were only two days left. To hell with it. She was out of there.

Jewell whirled around, ready to storm off, but was stopped in her tracks when Blake grabbed her arm and began walking toward one of the terrace doors. She wanted to dig in her heels and refuse to accompany him, but she also wanted to avoid causing a scene. This entire evening had been a nightmare, and her deepest wish right now was to scurry away into some dark corner and hide for a long, long time while she licked her wounds.

When she and Blake were alone, he pushed her up against the balcony railing, his laughter dying away as he looked down into her eyes. Her breath hitched.

"I shouldn't have laughed, Jewell. I'm actually surprised I did. But I didn't think twice about Monica being here. I've known her since I was about ten years old, and she's probably my best friend, as well as my personal assistant. The only woman I trust, actually."

"That doesn't mean she's not also your lover." Jewell fought the need to squirm after saying that.

"Well, considering she's married to one of the starting linebackers for the Seahawks, it pretty much does mean she's not my lover," Blake said with another chuckle.

It took a few moments for his words to sink in and then she felt like a complete and utter fool. But how was she to know they weren't intimate? She'd watched them all through dinner, and the two of them had shared jokes, laughter, easy touches… just like best friends did. And now she'd shown him that she cared. Dammit!

He moved even closer to her. "I have to admit that I like this jealous side of you, even if it's completely unfounded."

"I wasn't jealous. I just don't like feeling like a third wheel." Sheesh. Why didn't she sound convincing even to herself?

"I think you're lying. I should certainly punish you for that," he told her before leaning down and capturing her lips.

It didn't take long for Jewell to forget all about her jealousy and to focus solely on the amazing effect Blake had on her body.

When he allowed her to come up for air, he spoke to her in a serious voice. "Jewell, you should be very careful with what you show to the world. There are people who can use your emotions against you."

She went still as she looked at him. Who was he warning her against? Himself? Others? She really had no idea.

"I can take care of myself," she said, though a shiver ran

through her.

"I don't think you can, Jewell. I think you need someone to take care of you. Is that why you began working at Relinquish Control?"

She paused, trying to choose her words carefully. Maybe if he thought this, he would drop the subject. They had only two more days left, and he seemed to want to climb inside her head even more as the sand ran out of the hourglass.

"I have my reasons for working there," she said. "I don't honestly believe that you care. I think it's just your need to be in control."

"You're right, Jewell. I do need to be in control. You should remember that always, and know that I will eventually get my way."

"Warning accepted," she told him as he pulled her against his hard body again.

"I don't think you really know what that means, Jewell. Right now, I still own you."

"You never let me forget that, Blake."

"I don't understand, then, why I need to keep reminding you."

"Maybe because of your own insecurities," she was bold enough to say, making him tense up in her arms.

"You *will* push me too far one of these times."

She had no doubt that was true. What she didn't understand was her sudden desire to go back to his place. There really had to be something seriously wrong with her.

CHAPTER TWENTY-SIX

J EWELL PEEKED AROUND her bedroom door, trying to hear whether there were any sounds in the house. When she heard nothing, she tiptoed from the room, hopeful Blake wasn't there.

She'd slept in his room again the night before, but had rushed to her own room as dawn was just breaking — not that he'd been in bed. He was always up early, and usually gone by the time she came downstairs, if only for a couple of hours.

She didn't know his routine on Saturdays, though, and he hadn't mentioned any plans either with or without her. No matter what, she had to get over to see her brother for their weekly visit, and there was no way she'd be able to explain her disappearance. She could say she needed a walk, needed to go shopping, or just have a break, but since he'd insisted that she not leave the apartment, sneaking around was certainly in her cards today. She was so lucky that he hadn't been checking on her with those evil cameras.

Worry wrinkled her brow when she slipped into the kitchen to find a full pot of coffee and a note from Blake. Yes, she had her cell with her for once, but even if he'd still been texting her a lot, she was so terrible at answering his messages that he must have resorted to writing notes. Pen and paper — how primitive!

> *Be ready by five. I had an emergency I had to*
> *run to, but when I get back, we're going out.*

Blake

What a blessed relief! She could easily steal away, visit her brother, and be back in plenty of time. No problem! Gathering her purse, but leaving her phone off, she walked from the apartment feeling lighter and happier than she had in weeks.

Justin would never understand if she didn't come to see him. And Blake was taking her back to Relinquish Control tomorrow anyway, so what did it matter if she was out for a few hours? There was no need for either him or Ms. Beaumont to know about her brother, because as soon as she had enough money saved, she would never see any of these people again.

She waited impatiently at the nearby bus stop and didn't take her first full breath until she was out of sight of Blake's ritzy apartment building. She hadn't even looked over her shoulder, too fearful she'd find him standing right there, piercing her with those eyes of his and demanding to know where she was going.

It took an hour, but finally she reached the place where her brother was staying, and, putting on a big smile, she knocked on the door. It seemed to take an eternity, but when the door finally opened, she could barely resist pushing past his foster mother to get to her brother.

"Is Justin ready to come out for our visit?"

"He's not feeling well today," the woman said, her eyes cold.

Jewell hated that Justin had to live here, and her determination grew even greater as she stood on the woman's threshold. "Then I'll just visit with him here," she said. She wasn't leaving until she saw Justin.

"I don't know if today's visit is a good idea."

"I wasn't asking for your opinion," Jewell told her. "The state has given me visitation on Saturdays and I *will* see my brother."

Jewell looked her in the eyes, making it clear that she refused to back down. With a deep scowl, the woman finally opened the door wider, and Jewell didn't hesitate to step inside.

"Justin," she called out, and the sound of her brother's feet running down the hallway was the sweetest music she could ever recall hearing.

Bracing herself for the impact, she pulled him easily into her arms, and he clung to her, holding her as if he would never let go. If only this could last forever.

"They said you might not come today," Justin said when he finally let go.

"Nothing on this earth would keep me away from you on our special days," she assured him, too angry even to look at the woman. He wasn't sick — she'd been lying. Why? Probably because she was a bitter, sadistic woman who wanted to use her brother for the measly paycheck the state gave her. Well, Jewell was trying to take him away and the woman must not like that.

"That's great — I missed you. Are we still going to the pizza place?"

"You bet we are, Bubby. We have three hours and we're going to have the best time ever." Jewell went over to the coat closet and pulled out his ratty jacket. She couldn't wait until he was back living with her and she had the money to give him the things he needed and wanted.

"I'm so glad you're here, Sissy. I've had a bad week," he said, his eyes filling with tears.

"Why has your week been bad?" The two of them headed

to the door, and Jewell didn't even acknowledge Justin's foster mother as they moved past her and left the house. *Foster?* Now that was a sick joke, almost as sick as the *mother* part of her name.

"Ms. Penny said that I was misbehaving too much, so she made me stay in my room all day for two days," he told his sister.

"Oh, Justin, that's not okay at all. I'll talk to your social worker." Jewell struggled to moderate her voice so she wouldn't upset him.

"I was crying for you the other night and she told me to shut up, said that I needed to start acting like a man, not a crybaby. I try not to cry, but sometimes I just miss you so much." His voice quiet, but his little fingers trembled beneath hers.

Jewell stopped and knelt down on the sidewalk so she could see her little brother's face and he could see hers. "Sometimes emotions are just too much for us to bear and we have to release them. Don't ever let anyone tell you that what you are feeling isn't real. If you have to cry, then you do it, and just know that in five more Saturdays we're going to be together always and not just for a few hours at a time." She gave him another hug.

"You promise, Sissy. I don't want to be at Ms. Penny's house anymore. She's just so mean — nothing like how mama was."

"I promise you that no matter what I have to do, I will get you out of there, and you'll come to live with me. You have to just give it a little more time and be my brave little man, but not for much longer."

"I know I'm supposed to be brave, but it's so hard…" He stopped speaking when his voice began to choke up.

"You are brave, Justin. You keep holding your head up high and know that I am doing whatever it takes for us to be together. I got a job, a really good job, and I'm saving lots of money so we can have a beautiful place together, where we can put up pictures of mom, and where, if you need to cry, you can do so without any fear of being made fun of. We're a family and that means we stick together. No one can keep us apart for long, Bubby."

"I know. I say a prayer every single night, asking God to let me go home with you. Why does it take so long for Him to answer my prayer?"

Her heart broke in so many pieces, she didn't think it would ever be healed again. Her own eyes filled and a tear fell down her cheek. "Sometimes it takes a little longer because there are so many people out there needing so much, but you haven't been forgotten about — I promise you that."

Justin fell silent, perhaps afraid, despite his sister's reassurance, that too much talking would betray his emotions. He just held on tight and soon they began walking again. Jewell had to keep her promise, no matter what it meant for her, and no matter what would come next. She couldn't let her brother down.

After dropping her brother back at the foster home, she rushed to the bus stop and chewed her nails during the long ride. But that was silly. There was still plenty of time. Blake wouldn't even know she'd been gone. Still, she had a presentiment of doom when she got off the bus and rushed down the street toward his apartment building.

Once the front door opened, Jewell took a step back. Blake was sitting in a chair there in his entry hall, glaring daggers at her. This wasn't going to be pleasant.

He didn't say a word as she walked in. Nevertheless, she maintained an expression of poise and confidence, though her body shook with terror. She had only one more night left with him. Tonight. What could he really do?

When he stood up and took a menacing step toward her, she figured she was about to find out.

CHAPTER TWENTY-SEVEN

GAZING INTO BLAKE'S frigid eyes, Jewell tried to tell herself to be strong, tried to assure herself this was only one more bump in the road. He wouldn't hurt her physically — not that anyone would care if he did. After all, she'd signed releases at Relinquish Control, and she knew he could do with her what he wanted.

Though he might think she was nothing but a money-hungry whore, *she* still knew who she was. The cold fury in his expression was the only thing that was shaking her up. She'd never seen a man so angry before. His mouth remained in a hard line; not a muscle moved on his chiseled face.

"Where were you?"

Ice ran through her veins at his words, spoken quietly yet harshly. Yes, *fury* didn't even begin to describe what the man appeared to be feeling.

"I needed to get out of the apartment for a while, so I took a walk." Should she try to move past him or not? She thought the safest thing would be to stay right where she was.

"You're lying to me." She waited for him to say more, but

nothing else came from his tightly pressed lips.

"Do you have any idea how stir-crazy I get when I'm stuck here all day with very little to do? No, you probably don't, because you leave here at the crack of dawn. I will say this again — I needed to get out and walk off my 'cabin fever.'" She was trying desperately not to change her story.

He took a sinister step forward. "I spoke to McKenzie. She said you disappeared last Saturday as well. Is there a man you're meeting every Saturday, Jewell? Don't you dare lie to me!"

His voice rose just a little, but that was enough to show her he was barely in control. Maybe she shouldn't have come back to his place. It looked as if this wasn't going to go well for her — not well at all.

She didn't know what to say to his unfounded and totally unexpected accusation. But she was damned if she were going to stand there and take his verbal beating. If she stood her ground, refused to back down, refused to allow him to intimidate her, then wouldn't he stop? Isn't that what she'd been taught years before when she'd taken a self-defense class?

"Look, I wasn't with another man, Blake. I swear to that, and anyway, that makes no sense. You know I was a virgin before you. I just had something I needed to do today, and it's something that I can't talk about." She moved forward and edged by him, but made sure not to bow her head.

He didn't grab her, didn't try to stop her. That was a positive. She walked into the living room and went straight to the couch, afraid to stand any longer for fear that her legs would end up buckling.

"I don't believe you, Jewell. You may have been a virgin, but there are a lot of ways to get off. There had to have been someone pretty damn special for you to sneak out of my place to meet with him. Did you try to save yourself for him? Or was he the one who made you become a little whore?"

He came closer but still kept about five feet of distance between them. Was it because he feared he would forget his self-mastery if he touched her? That sent a shiver of fear down her spine. She wanted to spit in his face and tell him exactly what she thought, but she decided to be more judicious.

"I'm sorry if you don't believe me, but there's not another man. I neither want nor need a relationship with anyone, and that includes you. Your suspicions are simply stupid, and if you were as smart as you think you are, you should know that. Anyway, I leave here tomorrow and go back to Relinquish Control, and we can forget all about each other and what happened over the past few days."

There. Maybe pointing out the fact that they weren't in a relationship would change his attitude. Yes, he sort of owned her this week, but their time was pretty much up, and she owed this man nothing. She'd done everything he'd asked of her and more. A few more times with other men and she could get away from this place, leave Seattle even, and she and Justin could live happily — just the two of them.

If the state tried to keep him from her, she would take him away in the middle of the night and the two of them would go somewhere no one would ever find them. Alaska seemed far enough away. Maybe. It was still in the U.S. and if they were found, Washington state officials might still try to take her brother back, but would they search that far? She could live in some Eskimo village. It didn't matter as long as they were together.

"Follow me." He turned, confident that she would do as he said.

"One more night," she whispered to herself as she got up off the couch and walked behind him to the back of the apartment, where his office was.

As soon as she stepped through the door, her throat tightened. This was all his domain, where he spent his time when he wasn't away at work or in the bedroom. She knew he was coming in there because this was his fortress, his place of power.

If he wanted to intimidate her, he was doing a damn fine job.

She couldn't help but notice that it was more decorated than the rest of the place; it boasted expensive artwork, hardwood floors, and antique furniture. But no clutter was permitted in this space, making it in that way consistent with the rest of the house.

"Sit down, Jewell."

He indicated a stiff leather chair in the corner, but she didn't want to sit, didn't want him towering over her. Yes, her knees were still shaky, but she wasn't sure she'd be able to get up this time if she sat back down. She was on the verge of collapsing and she just needed to get away from him.

"I'd really like to take some Advil and lie down before we go out," she told him, staying where she was, just a few feet inside the door. "I have a terrible headache."

"You can't seem to listen, can you?"

He came closer to her. She wanted to retreat but she willed herself not to. Retreat would show him how weak she really was.

"I do listen. I've done everything that you've asked of me. I just…I won't allow you to attack me when I've done nothing to deserve it."

Her words stopped him, and his eyes widened, as if he was surprised that anyone would argue with him. She knew she shouldn't do it, but what else was she supposed to do? He was a large man and he was scaring the heck out of her.

"You *haven't* done everything I've asked. I asked that you stay in today. I asked you to get ready. Instead, you disappear — something it seems you like to do on Saturdays." As he spoke, his lips weren't nearly as hard as before.

"I wasn't doing anything wrong." Maybe if she said it enough, he'd finally understand and let her be.

"You will tell me where you went," he said, punctuating every word.

His voice had risen, and he was back in confrontational mode. When he moved right in front of her and faced her down, she wanted to take a step back, but she wasn't going to cower.

"You might as well take me back to Relinquish Control right now, because I won't tell you." Whatever was going to happen would happen. It was beyond her control.

"Fine!" He grabbed her arm and hustled her out of his office, down the hall, and right to the elevator door.

"What are you doing?"

"You want to go back? I'm taking you back. And you realize, of course, that I'll do my best to see that you won't get paid a dime for this week. I already know that McKenzie told you if I wasn't satisfied, you would lose your job, so you just screwed yourself. Remember that! This is all on you."

Bile rose in her throat. She was doing all of this for Justin, and because she'd visited him today, she'd be one step further back in her ability to have him permanently.

Tears burned in her eyes as she desperately tried to find some sort of explanation that would calm Blake's temper. But the man seemed to know when she was lying. He'd figure it out, and then he would still take her back. So instead of crying, instead of throwing up, she stood in silence beside Blake as they rode down and walked into the garage.

When he went to a large black pickup truck, she didn't know what to think. Blake drove expensive sports cars, not trucks that seemed more fitting for work. Then she remembered he'd been called to work and had most likely been using it on a job. That's what happened when they left Bill's house a few days ago.

Still, why was he taking her in it now? Why not just leave it? Maybe because there was a shovel in the back and he needed to take her in the truck and get rid of the evidence…

As Blake closed the passenger door and then entered the truck on the driver's side, Jewell focused on the windshield and the view straight in front of her. He was taking her back. She would get the paycheck — she didn't buy his threat that she wouldn't get a dime — and the first thing she was going to do was put down money on that apartment for her and her brother. Because as of tonight she would no longer have a job.

Yes, Ms. Beaumont would be furious, but even if she lost her job, she'd have enough to secure a place and some of the basics, enough to convince the courts that her brother should be with her and not strangers. She would get another job. There wasn't another choice.

A strange sense of peace washed over her, and Jewell turned to look out the side window. Soon this would all be over. Soon, she would be with her brother and both of their lives could return to something like a normal existence.

It was the only thing she could think. Because the alternative would send her into a downward spiral of depression she was sure she would never be able to escape.

CHAPTER TWENTY-EIGHT

RAGE ROLLED FROM Blake in never-ending waves. That feigned innocence he kept seeing in her eyes couldn't conceal the lies she was now telling him. He would get to the truth, and he would get to it tonight. If she seriously thought he was giving up, she had a lot left to learn about the real world.

Blake knew better than to touch her right now, though. He was angry enough that he was afraid of physically hurting her. That was ridiculous, of course — he would never hit her, never lose control. He was made of ice. How many people had said that about him?

He'd lost count.

Only his brothers were allowed in, and only because of the horror the three of them shared. It was them against the world. So why was he letting this woman, this insignificant woman, affect his moods?

As he pointed his truck away from the city, he watched her stealthily. Absurdly enough, he wanted to reach across the seat and haul her to his side. Her tantalizing scent was surrounding him, muddying his thoughts completely. In such a short time she had changed him in ways he didn't understand.

What he should do was take her back right away, drop her at the doors of Relinquish Control, just as he'd said he would, and never look back. He knew that wasn't going to happen just yet though. He needed to drive, needed to think before he dropped her off. Make her talk to him.

When he started down a road with no streetlights just as the sun left the sky, she turned toward him. Her face was barely visible in the insignificant light from the dash, but he had no doubt she was worried. Good. Let her worry. She had caused him an unbearable rush of emotion today. She could deal with fear.

About ten miles out in the middle of nowhere, she finally spoke, her voice quavering. "This isn't the way back to Relinquish. Where are we going?"

"You'll find out." His tone was still harsh, his feelings still barely under control. No. He couldn't touch her yet, but soon… Yes, he'd soon be touching her a whole hell of a lot.

"Blake—"

She broke off, and he had no idea what she was going to say, because just then he heard a loud thumping noise followed by the sound of his tire shredding.

"Dammit!" Blake yanked his foot off the gas and eased the truck over to the side of the road. They were miles from anywhere, in the middle of mint fields, the aroma everywhere.

His first instinct was to call his assistant, get someone out there to fix the truck so he could take her where he'd planned. Then, as he lifted his phone and was about to press the buttons, he had second thoughts.

Yes, rage still filled him, but desire was even stronger. "Come here, Jewell."

The dash lights were their only illumination, but he easily saw the shiver that raced through her body at his words. He had no doubt she would follow his orders.

That was what gave her the advantage. He was waiting for her to climb over to him, and instead, she threw open the passenger side door and bolted from the truck. He sat there dumbfounded for a minute, then jumped from the vehicle. Both of the truck doors were now wide open, and the light glowing from the truck offered him some slight assistance in his chase, and yet her shadow was barely visible as she sprinted away.

"Get back here," he thundered, then silently rebuked himself. The tone of his voice wasn't going to reassure her, persuade her to stop, and if she didn't, he knew he'd lose her in the dark.

Throwing off his custom suit jacket, not caring where it landed, he ran after her. As it turned out, she didn't stand a chance. She hadn't made it very far when he caught up to her and lifted her into his arms. Her scream floated away into the night.

"Stop now!" he told her as he turned and began making his way back to the truck with her struggling in his arms.

"Don't do this, Blake. I'm sorry, but I can't tell you where I was. I wasn't doing anything that would dishonor you, I swear."

"I don't care. You *will* tell me, but we'll revisit that later," he said in a steady voice as they reached the truck.

"What are you going to do?"

He sat her on the hood of the truck, spread her legs, and moved up against her, aligning his face perfectly with hers.

"Whatever I want." With that, he grasped her neck and pulled her close, sealing their mouths together and only beginning to scratch the surface of his hunger where this woman was concerned.

She struggled for several moments, until he gentled his hold, his anger draining and seduction taking its place. Only then did she melt against him, a whimper escaping her throat as he broke through the barrier of her lips and plundered her mouth, making sure she thought of no other man but him.

Wrapping his arms around her as he dominated her in the best way he knew how, he pushed away the thoughts of who was really in control here. He was transported to a place where his problems evaporated, where the endless void of his life paradoxically disappeared. Nothing mattered when he was in her arms, when his lips were on hers, when his body sank inside her. Nothing mattered but her.

Only passion, heat, and lust were real in this moment. Only Jewell was real.

When he broke the kiss, he couldn't see her face — the light from the truck was behind her. He could only hear her deep, panting breaths as he reached for the hem of her shirt and began tugging on it. He needed to feel her skin, needed to taste every single inch of her body.

He slid his fingers over her taut stomach, and its muscles shook underneath his touch, making him feel stronger, invincible, even. Her gasp of pleasure when his fingers glided over her full breasts and peaked nipples sent a shock wave through him.

Still, she wore too many clothes! He carefully pushed her backward, laying her flat on the hood of his truck, and he put his hands under the waistband of her jeans and undid them, then dragged them and the thin piece of silk covering her womanhood down off her trembling legs.

He smoothed his hands up her thighs and past her stomach, and cupped her sweet breasts, making her groan with need. Her response to him made him ache unbearably.

His manhood pulsed, and he was ready to strip off his

clothes and take her right then, to plunge within her heat, to feel the walls of her core pulse around him. But he wouldn't rush this. No.

His brow beaded with sweat. He drew back long enough only to rip his shirt buttons open and fling the offending garment on the ground.

The cloud cover cleared and the light from the full moon gave him a perfect view of her ivory flesh against his dark truck, and the sight of her nearly made him fall to his knees in appreciation. When she looked up, took in his chest and let out a little gasp, he didn't know how he remained on his feet.

"I want you now. I want you always. I can't get enough of you," he said as he undid his pants and pushed them down, leaving him bare before her.

The frustration in her greedy eyes fueled his desire even further, and he came up to her again and ran his hands along the inside of her spread thighs. But when goose bumps appeared on her flesh, he stopped.

"Are you cold?" The air was warm and he was burning up, but maybe making love out in the open wasn't the best idea.

"No," she whispered with a shake of her head, her voice barely audible.

"Are you scared?" He held his breath and waited.

"Not at all," she said. It wasn't fear that was causing her to shake all over.

Her answer filled him with pride. He'd been happy to see her frightened earlier — he'd been furious — but when it came down to it, he didn't want her afraid of him; he wanted her to desire him, need him, not want to let him go.

Even though that was against the rules.

Blake was beginning to hate the rules set between them, hate how this had all started. In only a week, she had taken hold of something inside him, though he wasn't sure what and wasn't about to analyze it. No. This was about sex, and only sex.

"I won't hurt you, Jewell. No matter how angry I am, I would never hurt you." He needed her to know this, and needed her to tell him she believed that. She was silent and he waited, his hands resting just beneath her heat as he throbbed before her.

"Please, Blake. I need you," she told him.

"No, Jewell. Tell me you know I won't hurt you," he demanded. He slid his hands up her body, stopping them just below the rise and fall of her breasts before moving back down to her core, circling her most sensitive area.

"Blake…"

He said nothing, but rubbed his arousal against her leg, letting her know that he was more than ready for her.

"I know you won't hurt me," she finally gasped in frustration. "Please, please touch me."

He didn't need to hear anything beyond that. He moved one hand lower, pressing his fingers inside of her while the other trailed up her body and moved over the mound of her breast and up over her nipple, making her arch her back and groan once more into the night.

Lowering his head, he pulled her closer to him, then took her peaked nipple in his mouth and sucked, flicking his tongue over the ridge as she moved beneath him.

"More, please, more," she begged, reaching out tugging on his hair, holding him tightly against her.

"Here?" he teased as he lifted his mouth, moved across her perfect mounds and flicked his tongue over her other nipple, wetting it with his hot mouth.

"Yes!" she cried out, grasping at him, clutching him, telling him with her movements that she wanted his skin against hers, his body sunk deep inside.

He wasn't ready to do that yet. He'd go wild and wouldn't be able to give her the pleasure she deserved, so he drew back from her grasp and trailed his mouth down the tight curve of her stomach. Urged on by her trembling, he skimmed his mouth across her heat.

At the first swipe of his tongue, her body jumped from the truck. Tucking his hands beneath her luscious backside, he held her in place as he spread her core and licked along her sweet walls.

Pressing his mouth against her pulsing core, he sucked the tender flesh of her engorged bud, and he gloried in her cries of release that engulfed him. He still couldn't get enough of her.

"I need to take you, Jewell — now. I want to make you mine over and over again," he said, though he didn't think too deeply about those words. He drew her to him, catching her body in his arms as he lined them up together, his throbbing manhood begging for entrance.

Before thrusting inside her, he captured her bottom lip tenderly and sucked it into his mouth, absorbing the gasp she let out, all the while caressing her back with his hands. Now he pressed closer, and the head of his arousal slipped inside her swollen heat.

He found her pulse beating strongly in the scented skin of her neck, mint drifting all around them, suddenly becoming his favorite herb ever, and then he licked her flesh, knowing he would never get enough of her taste, enough of her body, enough of any of this.

She moved against him, her body twisting to get closer as the flames of desire quickly built back up within her. She wanted him to feel her, and he wasn't going to deny her any longer.

His thick length rested intimately just inside her, but he pulled back to look into her eyes before he pushed forward in a slow, sure thrust that had him coming unglued.

When she sank her teeth into the side of his neck, he nearly spilled his seed right then. "Hold on," he gasped, trying to regain control over his body. That seemed to encourage her to push him to his very limits.

Bringing her head upward, he closed his mouth over hers, his kiss hungry, desperate, full of want and need and emotion he couldn't identify.

He didn't try to hold back any longer, but plunged in and out of the safety of her body, propelling them both higher and higher, their groans filling the night skies, their passion seemingly infinite.

He fought for self-control, fought to slow down, but it was no use. Her legs circled his back, and he drove deeper, faster, harder, until he heard her cry out, felt her body tense around him and convulse in explosive ecstasy.

Pleasure then rushed through him, and he cried out too, his body pulsing within hers, his pleasure complete as he pumped deep inside her tight sheath. The shudders of both their bodies didn't soon die down.

When their breathing finally approached normal, she lifted her head, showing him eyes bright and cheeks still rosy from her release. "I guess that was a nice ending to our week." Her voice was slightly shy, though she was trying to say the words almost like a joke.

He wasn't in the mood for laugher.

"I guess you're right," he said, and, withdrawing from her body, felt instantly empty.

He helped her from the truck and she stood there naked and trembling before him.

"What are you going to do now, Blake?"

"Since you refuse to tell me the truth, our time is over."

He turned and picked up his pants, slipping them on before going to get the spare tire from the back of the truck. She dressed in silence and climbed inside the cab. He had no idea what she was feeling because she was quickly learning to make her face a mask.

What he didn't understand was the tightening in his chest. As he got into the truck and made his way back to the city, he felt his pulse beating strongly. When they reached the back doors of Relinquish Control, he stepped from the truck, his face cold and unforgiving as he rang the buzzer.

McKenzie stepped out, her surprise obvious from her face. "Blake, you're early," she exclaimed. Then she immediately composed herself.

"Ms. Weston hasn't worked out," he said, no emotion coming through in his tone.

"What do you mean? Your time is up in the morning," she told him.

"She didn't follow the rules. I'm finished with her."

McKenzie said nothing else as she held open the door for Jewell to step through, and when it clicked shut behind them, Blake found himself wanting to bust right through. But with iron control, he instead moved to his truck and stepped up into the driver's seat.

And drove away…

EPILOGUE

WHEN MAX STEPPED inside Blake's apartment Monday morning, he knew something had to be wrong with his boss. No one had heard from the man since Saturday, and that had never happened before. He was always available, if only by phone. The driver was almost afraid of what he was going to find.

When he made his way to the living room, he saw Blake sprawled out on the couch wearing only a pair of sweats and with at least two days' growth of beard on his face. The smell of expensive Scotch hung heavy in the air.

Slowly approaching, he shook his boss's shoulder lightly and was relieved to hear the man emit a groan. Max went off to the kitchen and made a fresh pot of coffee, then poured a cup and returned to the living room. He now shook Blake until he woke up.

"What are you doing?" Blake grumbled as he sat up with some effort and shot Max a vicious glare.

"I think the bigger question is, what are you doing?" his driver countered.

"It's none of your damn business, Max. If I wanted company, I would have called," Blake said. He grabbed the cup of coffee and downed half of it before wincing when he felt the hot liquid scorch his throat.

"Is this about Jewell?" Max asked boldly, and was rewarded with another glare.

"No woman has the power to affect me," Blake snarled.

"I followed her on Saturday," Max said, and the room went completely silent.

Max could see that Blake was wondering why he hadn't thought sooner to ask his employee whether he'd done that. It could have saved him a lot of misery.

"And?" Blake obviously wasn't in the mood for suspense.

"She was obviously sneaking off somewhere. I knew you would want to know where. You know, I actually find myself liking the girl," Max said with a chuckle.

"I don't give a damn if you like her," Blake thundered. "Tell me where she went."

"She went to a house — by bus, if you're interested — and then emerged with a boy, a young boy. They went to a pizza place, and then three hours later, she returned him. I was going to talk to you and find out if you wanted me to find out who the boy is."

Max waited, surprised when he saw the little color in his boss's face drain wholly away. He had no idea what that meant, so he waited, knowing Blake was processing his words.

"She was telling me the truth…"

While Max looked at him blankly, Blake stared silently at the floor. Then, when his boss stood up and moved to the stairs, the driver remained where he was. He didn't know what was coming next.

Blake and Jewell's story isn't finished yet. See the conclusion in *Broken*, coming out December 15th, 2014. Available for pre-order now at

Amazon - iBooks

PREVIEW OF SURRENDER
BY MELODY ANNE

Available now

*Having everything to lose
can make a person
do desperate things.*

*Would you surrender to
help the one you love?*

PROLOGUE

DIVORCE.

His throat closed up at the mere thought of that word. He was twenty-eight years old and had conquered the universe — or thought he had.

No! He had.

Then his picture-perfect world had shattered with a single word.

Divorce.

He'd been respectable and respectful, always treating women with admiration. He hadn't jumped into marriage at twenty-one, but had dated the same woman for three years, had cherished her, had given her everything. He thought he'd found perfection, but found disillusion instead.

Raffaello Palazzo sat straight up; his eyes narrowed.

No! He wasn't this man.

Even if groveling had been in his nature, which it most assuredly wasn't, he wouldn't consider doing it now.

"Goodbye."

He barely glanced up as Sharron walked past, her five-thousand-dollar purse slung over her shoulder, and flaunted the smirk on her face as she slammed the door in all finality. She was gone, and he was grateful.

A couple of her complaints against him were that he worked too much and he wasn't as attentive as she thought she deserved.

When he'd walked in the week before with a bouquet of roses, attempting to give her the attention she'd demanded, he'd seen that she wasn't choosy about the source of the attention. She'd been in bed with his business partner. Then, to add insult to injury, she'd attempted to take him for all he was worth.

She'd lost.

Rafe's eyes closed as he pictured that horrible afternoon.

"Are you cutting out on us?"

"It's my anniversary. I had my wife's favorite flower, the Hawaiian Flora, delivered express to the floral shop, and I'm picking up her bouquet, then taking her on a surprise trip to Paris. That's where we celebrated our honeymoon."

"You're the most whipped man I know, Rafe," his assistant, Mario Kinsor, said with a smile.

"I'm half Italian. My father learned the ways of my mother's country and how gallant the men are and he taught me how to cherish a woman," Rafe replied genially, not offended in the least. He hoped to have as strong a marriage as his parents had, and for just as long.

"When does Ryan get back? If you're cutting out, I'll need one of the business partners here to get work done."

"He's flying in on Friday. I spoke to him a few days ago, and he said he met someone. I'm looking forward to meeting her."

"I can't take any more of this mushy talk. Get out of

here before your lovesickness becomes contagious. I'll see you Monday."

"Night, Mario. Thanks for all your hard work this week."

Heading for the door, Rafe waved to his faithful assistant. Life was great — his corporation was flourishing without help from his family, and his personal life couldn't be better.

It didn't take Rafe long to breeze into the florist's and then arrive home. When he couldn't find Sharron downstairs, he smiled in anticipation. Maybe she was stretched out on their bed in a sexy nightie…

When Rafe opened the door, he did find her in bed, and scantily dressed — hell, not dressed at all — but she wasn't alone. He froze as shock filled him.

"Ohhh, Ryan!" Sharron cried out, and Rafe's illusions of happily ever after shattered.

Silently, he stood in the dim light as one of his two best friends screwed his wife. It had been Ryan, Shane and him since middle school, always sharing — always there for one another. Rafe guessed Ryan figured Rafe's wife was included in what Rafe was willing to share. Wrong.

Rafe cleared his throat as Sharron screamed again in pleasure. The two of them froze — locked in their torrid embrace — before their heads turned and they looked at him in horror.

Rafe walked from the room and waited downstairs. Almost immediately, Ryan scurried from the house with his head down. Sharron rushed toward Rafe and started to beg for his forgiveness.

Rafe shook off the unpleasant memory as he glanced around him. For a single moment, he'd been shattered. He'd sacrificed so much of himself to please her — give her what she wanted — but none of that was enough. She'd wanted everything from him — namely all his net worth. He wouldn't make the same mistake twice; he never did.

Rafe walked up the steps and stood just inside the bedroom door, looking warily around at the room where he'd slept beside that woman night after night. Shaking his head, he left and made his way toward his luxury kitchen. No memories lingered there. It wasn't as though his wife had known the first thing about cooking.

He had a full staff, which was a good thing. Otherwise his house would have been in shambles and he'd never have gotten fed. Sharron hadn't been domestic in the least. He hadn't cared about that — all he'd wanted was to have the same kind of family life with her as the one he'd grown up with. Before this moment, he'd been under the sad delusion that marriages could all have happy endings.

A cold silence hung around him like a shroud, and Rafe was grateful he'd sent his staff away for the day. He didn't need anyone witnessing his failure.

Failure.

He rolled the word around on his tongue. It didn't sound right. How could it? Failure was a foreign concept to him. He'd been born with the proverbial silver spoon in his mouth. And his mother often teased him, saying he was an old soul in a young body.

She was the *only* one who could get away with a remark like that — he adored her. Well, to be fair, his sisters got away with it, too, and for the same reason.

Rafe had a sudden feeling that all his family members would be relieved to hear of the coming divorce, especially his mother, though she'd never admit it to him. She had tried to get close to his soon-to-be ex-wife, but somehow it had never happened. Had Sharron had any desire at all to know his family? Now that he thought of it, he couldn't recall any evidence in her favor. True, he wouldn't have noticed while the two of them were dating, because that was during the six months out of the year that his family resided in Italy. By the time his parents and sisters had returned for their six months in California, he and Sharron were already married.

And then? It hit him right in the gut. From the very beginning, Sharron had been great at making up excuses for why she couldn't visit with them. But he was in love and stupid and he just hadn't noticed. If he had, he would never have become so serious about her. He'd been raised to believe that family always came first. Upon their marriage, he'd put her first, just as his father had put his mother first. Soon, he'd cut down on visiting his family —she'd said she couldn't go, and he wanted to please her by remaining with her. He'd done a lot of things to make the woman happy.

Apparently none of it had been enough.

With a last glance around the kitchen, he lifted his cell phone and dialed. His call was picked up on the other end of the line before the phone could ring twice.

"Sell the house. I want nothing in it," Rafe said to his assistant in clipped tones.

"Yes, sir." There was no arguing. Mario had been an employee of his from the day Rafe had started his billion-dollar corporation. The man was loyal, efficient, and trustworthy. Rafe couldn't imagine how much harder his job would have become without his favorite employee.

Rafe had learned everything from his dad, Martin Palazzo, who had made millions in the stock market, and later in smart real-estate investments. Martin had met Rosabella, Rafe's mother, while traveling for business in Italy. The two of them had been inseparable ever since, but Rosabella couldn't stand to stay away from her homeland for more than six months at a time, which was why Rafe had spent half his childhood in Italy and half in the States.

Because of his multicultural upbringing, he was much more prepared to take on the global business structure he'd adopted. He was a fierce businessman and loyal to the end to those he loved. After today, trust would be something he held much closer to his heart and gave only with caution.

Rafe had decided from an early age that he needed to make his own way in life — not just have everything handed to him by his wealthy parents. He wasn't stupid, though. He'd taken his father's advice, had even done business with him, but Rafe had dreamed big — and turning that dream into reality had taken him much less time than it would have taken the average person.

Whenever he walked into his twenty-five-story office building in San Francisco, he felt a justified pride. He created jobs for hundreds of thousands of people throughout the world, gave them an income, made sure they went to bed each night with a full stomach and the security of more work to be done in the morning.

He gave so much — and unlike his soon-to-be ex-wife, his employees were grateful and regarded him almost as a king. Sharron had thrown everything he'd given her right back in his face. Except for money.

Rafe was finished with women. *Well*, he thought with an arrogant smirk, *finished with playing the good guy*. It was his turn to take what he wanted. Never again would he be used — never again would he put his heart out there to be carelessly trampled on. It seemed all women had a purpose, and it was fueled by their greed. The richer the man, the better for them. They wanted to be taken care of, and they all had their price.

Walking purposefully out his front door, he'd refused to even turn around to watch the final latching of the lock. When he was through with something, it was over. He was done with this house.

Placing his hand on the cool metal handle on the door of his black Bentley, he barely heard the familiar click as the catch released. And as he climbed into the seat, he was oblivious to the fresh, pungent smell of the smooth leather upholstery.

Pulling quickly out of the driveway, Rafe began heading the short distance to the city, where he had a condo a couple of blocks from his office building. Luckily, Sharron had refused to live in San Francisco, causing him to sleep there on the many late nights he'd worked. The apartment was his — his alone.

If she'd so much as touched the doorway of the roomy penthouse, he'd have sold it as well. He wanted no reminders of the woman, nothing of her to remain in his life. He wanted a fresh slate. To have the last eight years back — that's what he wanted most of all, but since that was impossible, he'd simply have to erase her completely from his life from this day forward.

A few more phone calls and that would be done.

CHAPTER ONE

Three years later

Y OU'RE TOO THIN."
Arianna Harlow trembled as the man prowled around her, continuously circling her chair. She felt like a caged animal just waiting for him to strike. Why was she still sitting there? Why didn't she say the job wasn't for her, that it had all been a big mistake and she'd best be on her way?

She knew why. Reality flooded her mind — why she couldn't afford to walk away — that was, *if* he offered her the job. She was barely staying above water with her bills overflowing. Her mother was about to be moved from the rehabilitation home she was in, shipped to a lesser facility, and Ari didn't have a dollar left in her bank account.

She was truly afraid. If her mother were sent to the state care facility, she'd probably wither away to nothing and in no time at all. Ari couldn't let that happen — she wouldn't.

Arianna had already dropped out of school during her last semester, her life forever changed because of one brief moment in time, because of one horrendous mistake.

If only...

Those two words had haunted her thoughts for the past six months. She had several different endings to those words, but the dominant words were *if only...*

If only she hadn't called her mom in panic that night.

If only she hadn't gone to the party in the first place.

If only her mother had left a few minutes later.

"Are you listening to me?" Raffaello Palazzo's voice rumbled through the air, causing Ari to jump in her seat. She had to think for a moment about what he'd last said to her. Oh, yeah, she was too thin.

"Yes, Mr. Palazzo. I just don't know how to respond to that."

"Hmm." His voice came out as a hum, drifting across her nerve endings. Rafe was incredibly intimidating as he paced back and forth, towering over her at a few inches above six feet. Add to that his jet-black hair and stunning eyes and she felt like a rumpled factory worker, totally out of her element in this exquisite office.

As he made another pass around the room and neared her, Ari thought back over the last week — how strange it had been. Never before had she jumped through such hoops during a job interview.

She'd applied for more than a hundred jobs in the past month, and only three employers had called her back. One job had been at a bank; the manager had called her a few days later, saying they'd given the position to another applicant. The second was at an insurance company, and they'd told her she didn't have enough experience.

The third job…well, she didn't really know how to describe what she'd been through. The ad had said only this:

Seeking full-time applicants for Palazzo Corporation. Must be willing to work seven days a week, long hours. Must have no other commitments — no family, second jobs, or school. Salary 100k a year plus expenses. Hand-delivered applications only.

Ari thought getting the job would be a long shot, but she had nothing to lose by applying. She had immediately spruced up her résumé, which only included two years in her local pizza parlor, then almost four years as a part-time secretary in the Stanford history department. And after that, nothing — a six-month gap in employment while she took care of her mother and dealt with the fallout of that disastrous night.

With only one semester away from graduation, her life had changed forever because of the first foolish mistake she'd ever made. Why had she been so careless with only a few short months to go? Now that night would haunt her, be something she'd have to live with for the rest of her life.

With a leather notebook in hand, résumé and application inside, she had entered the large building and approached the security guard in the lobby, who'd directed her to the secretary's office on the twenty-fifth floor. In she'd walked with what she hoped was confidence exuding from her every pore, and she'd handed over her polished résumé.

"Thank you, Ms. Harlow. If you'll have a seat, Mr. Kinsor will call you in shortly."

Oddly enough only women were in the room when Ari sat down, not a male applicant to be seen. The frightening part was that all of them looked far more qualified for whatever office position was open. One by one the women had stepped into a room, the door shutting behind them. After about ten minutes they'd walked back out, their expressions confident as they eyed the remaining applicants. This business world was a sharkfest and Ari didn't know if she was up for the swim.

"Ms. Harlow?"

"Right here," she'd called. Adjusting her oversized glasses, and picking at the bottom of her two-sizes-too-big shirt, she stood and walked resolutely toward the small man wearing a sharp business suit and gentle smile on his face.

"This way, please."

She'd followed him into a room where a blue screen was set against the wall. There was a table with a piece of paper and a pen sitting atop it and nothing more.

"Please have a seat. I'm going to take your picture."

Ari hadn't understood the need for a picture just yet. Possibly it was for an ID card or employee badge, but usually that was done after you were hired. Maybe they were running it through security to make sure she wasn't a criminal. It didn't matter. She wasn't going to protest.

She had taken her seat and waited for the flash, knowing her smile wasn't genuine, but her anticipation had been so high, it was impossible to offer anything bigger than a slight grimace.

"Please fill out this form and make sure all contact information is correct. If you've passed to the second part of our screening process, we'll call you in three to five days," Mr. Mario Kinsor had said with the same gentle smile.

He hadn't asked her whether she had any questions. He hadn't elaborated on the job. Normally, she would have just filled out the paperwork and kept silent, but her rising curiosity had pushed her with an unknown bravery to ask what the job actually was.

"Mr. Kinsor, the ad in the paper was vague. What exactly does this job entail?"

"If you make it to the next level, you'll be given more information, Ms. Harlow. I'm sorry, but Mr. Palazzo is a very private man and this position is…confidential," he'd answered with a slight pause.

"I understand," Ari had said with a brittle smile, though she hadn't understood at all.

She'd scanned the solitary paper on the table and her confusion had only worsened.

What are your hobbies?

Are you in a serious relationship? If not, when was the last one you were in?

Are you available to travel?

What kind of questions were these? Was the second one even allowed in a job interview? Still, she'd answered as best she could and finally read a question that made sense:

What are your career goals?

The sentence had elicited a genuine smile. Before her mother's car accident, before her life had changed so dramatically, she'd been an honors student at Stanford, working toward her bachelor's degree in history. She'd planned on getting her master's, then a doctorate so she could be a university professor.

Someday…

In her heart of hearts she still held out hope of resuming her life at some point — accomplishing the goals she'd set for herself. But instant guilt filled her whenever that hope entered conscious thought. Her mother would have liked to have her life back, too, but she never would. It was only fair that Ari make sacrifices. Ari had to atone for her sins.

Her mother had sacrificed for her entire life so that Ari could have what she needed. She'd paid for Ari's education at a small private school, and then she'd scrimped and saved to send her to the best college. Ari had earned scholarships, but her mother paid for her room and board and even her beloved car.

Ari had never realized how much her mother had given of herself until the day her mom had been checked into the hospital. Circumstances now demanded that Ari grow up quickly, without having her mother to lean on. She was now responsible for her mom's care — and Ari was failing at her new role in life.

Since the day of her mother's car accident, their lives had been filled with utter trepidation and uncertainty.

Thankfully, the Palazzo Corporation had called her back. But the second interview had been more odd than the first. She'd been put through a fitness test. They'd had her run on a treadmill for half an hour, timed her as she navigated an obstacle course, and then tested her endurance.

She'd run track all through high school and continued her running at college, so the physical aspect hadn't been a problem, but with each step she'd taken in the bizarre interview process, she'd felt rising concern about what she was applying for.

All they'd offered in response at the second interview was that it was a private position with the CEO of the corporation. Maybe she was expected to dodge bullets in countries he was invading? She'd heard rumors that his businesses weren't always welcome overseas — that some of the governments thought he was overstepping his bounds.

From the research Ari had done, the people normally welcomed him, as he paid high wages and offered excellent benefit packages. A lot of the time it seemed it was other businesses that wanted to keep him out because when he came in, he conquered, no matter what industry he was pursuing.

So she knew that if she got the job, she'd have security. People rarely quit when they worked for the Palazzo Corporation.

The pay for the position was high enough to give her mother good medical care and still leave enough left over for her to save up — possibly getting her back to school within a couple of years. At this point, she'd do almost anything to be hired.

"Ms. Harlow, if you aren't going to take this interview seriously, you may exit the way you came in," Mr. Palazzo said in an irritated tone, snapping her back to the present.

"I'm sorry. I truly am. I do take this interview *very* seriously," she quickly answered, hoping she hadn't missed a question.

"I won't repeat myself again — do you understand?" Before she could answer, he continued. "I asked if you're available all hours. I don't mean Monday through Friday. This job requires your availability to me seven days a week, night and day. There will be times I won't need you for extended periods, and other times I'll need you with me for several days straight. There may be travel involved. The bottom line is that you must have *zero* other commitments. If that doesn't work for you, this interview is over."

Ari felt a lump in the back of her throat as she struggled to hold in the tears threatening to spring to her eyes. She finally gazed into his unusually colored eyes, getting her first solid look at them.

She'd heard about his type of eyes before, with something called heterochromia iridis, where two colors were present. His had a deep purple center around the pupil, fading into a gorgeous midnight blue. They were mesmerizing — intriguing — capturing her gaze, even though they were narrowing intensely right then.

"I have no other commitments. I'm available," she told him, inwardly crossing her fingers. She was committed to her mother, but with this money she wouldn't have to worry about her mom's care. She'd go see her when she had those downtimes he was speaking of. If she didn't get in to see her mom for a month, she'd be devastated, but her mom would be in good hands, and, most importantly, she wouldn't notice since she was in a coma.

"What about your mother?" he asked, as if reading her mind, his gaze boring into hers. She was stunned by the question, leaving her silent for a couple of seconds too long.

"How do you know about my mom?"

"I know everything I need to know about you, Arianna," he replied with a slight lifting of the corner of his mouth.

His expression was *far* too knowing and she immediately felt the urge to flee. Something wasn't right; something was telling her to get out while she still could. She was in over her head — she could feel it. All signs pointed to jumping from the chair and rushing out his door. But no. Loyalty to her mother kept her seated where she was.

"Yes. Of course," she responded. "My mother is being well taken care of. She's not even aware of who I am at this point. It won't hurt her in the least if she doesn't see me for long stretches of time."

He circled her again, causing her foot to twitch. When she was nervous, she did one of two things — tapped her foot, much to the annoyance of everyone around her, or bit on her thumbnail. She felt the urge to raise her hand, to make contact between thumbnail and teeth, but with great mental effort she kept her hands folded in her lap.

"I can see that as a hindrance, but as she's the only family member you have, I'll let it slide for now."

Was this guy for real? He'd let it slide? Ari was taking in air through her nose in long, deep pulls to keep her temper at bay. She needed the job, she kept reminding herself as she clenched her fingers tightly and locked her jaw to keep the words she wanted to throw at him from rushing out.

"Is something upsetting you, Ms. Harlow?" he asked, his voice smooth as molasses as he came back around and looked into her eyes again. She felt as if he were analyzing her, breaking her down into parts, trying to decide whether she was a waste of his time or not. She was sure that was how he conducted all his business. It was most likely why he was where he was in life, at the top of the ladder, and why she was at the bottom.

Some people oozed pure confidence, the ability to command and conquer the universe, and Mr. Palazzo had that in spades. She'd have given her soul for just a piece of his winning attitude and unyielding faith in himself.

"Everything's fine, Mr. Palazzo," she replied, proud of how calm and level her voice sounded, especially since her nerves were fried.

"You intrigue me, Ms. Harlow. I see you try and hide beneath your ridiculously baggy clothes, and large glasses, but there's something about you that makes me want to find out what it is you don't want the world to see." He paused, making her tug on her blouse again. "I don't hesitate once I make a decision, and I've decided to hire you…temporarily. I can see that your temper might cause a problem, but then again, meek has never been my style. Obedient…yes, but not meek."

Ari gaped at him as she tried to decipher his words. What was he talking about? What did meek and obedient have to do with anything?

"You're aware you signed a nondisclosure agreement

before ever setting foot into my office, correct? Whatever is said by me is strictly confidential...and that *legal* agreement highly enforced. A former employee tried to go to the media — *once*. Let's just say, she's now lost everything...and the rumors were quickly squashed. I very much play hardball, Ms. Harlow, and it would behoove you to not become my enemy," he said in a conversational voice.

Ari swallowed hard as her eyes continued to follow him intently. He spoke of a woman's ruin as if he were absently mentioning what he had eaten for lunch the previous day. Did she really want to work for this man?

But honestly, what choice did she have?

"I'm aware of what I signed, Mr. Palazzo." Ari sat up straighter in her chair, the reality of obtaining the job starting to set in. She wasn't afraid of losing everything because she had nothing to lose. Besides that, she knew how to keep things private. It wasn't as though she had any girlfriends to gossip with, anyway. She'd always been too focused on school to keep friends. A few had come and gone in her life, but none had lasted the test of time, thinking she was far too boring for their liking.

Her one attempt at acting like a normal college student... the thought made her shudder. It was the reason she was stuck in an interview for a job she was afraid to know the title of, instead of sitting in class listening to her professor.

Rafe Palazzo's searing gaze fixed her to the spot. He'd said that he didn't go back once he made a decision, but the assessing look in his eyes belied his words. She could see that he was undecided whether he wanted actually to hire her.

She said a quick prayer that she hadn't blown this opportunity. Of course, her mother's words of advice as she'd dropped Ari off at the Stanford dorms for the first time flashed through her mind. Her mom had told her that, if the situation looks too good to be true, then it probably is, and you should run like hell in the other direction. Maybe she *should* start running, Ari thought.

"Very well, then, Ms. Harlow. The job position is for a mistress…my mistress, to be exact."

SURRENDER is available at all Major Retailers.